"I'm impressed by your courage," Rafe said. "The B and B owners here in Glory put everything at risk—even silly pranks can threaten your future. I couldn't handle the stress."

"So you chose a low-stress career—police work," Emma said.

"It's a different kind of stress," Rafe said with a smile. "Glory's mystery prankster, for example—I wish we had more leads."

Emma stopped, standing under a streetlight on Water Street. "Well," she said, "there's one lead we haven't considered yet."

To Rafe's surprise, Emma's "we" sounded perfectly appropriate.

"There's some sort of deeper connection between the latest prank and my bed-and-breakfast," she said.

RON AND JANET BENREY

Ron and Janet Benrey began writing romantic cozy mysteries together more than ten years ago—chiefly because they both loved to read them. Their successful collaboration surprised them both, because they have remarkably different backgrounds.

Ron holds degrees in engineering, management and law. He built a successful career as a nonfiction writer specializing in speechwriting and other aspects of business writing. Janet was an entrepreneur before she earned a degree in communications, working in fields such as professional photography, executive recruiting and sporting-goods marketing.

How do they write together and still stay married? That's the question that readers ask most. The answer is that they've developed a process for writing novels that makes optimum use of their individual talents. Perhaps even more important, their love for cozy mysteries transcends the inevitable squabbles that occur when they're writing.

Ron & Janet Benrey
Glory Be!

Steeple
Hill®

Published by Steeple Hill Books™

STEEPLE HILL BOOKS

Steeple
Hill®

ISBN-13: 978-0-373-44245-4
ISBN-10:   0-373-44245-9

GLORY BE!

www.SteepleHill.com

Printed in U.S.A.

Rejoice in the Lord always.
I will say it again: Rejoice!
Let your gentleness be evident to all.
The Lord is near.
—*Philippians* 4:4-5

For Collette and Craig Crandall.
Welcome to Glory!

ONE

"What's wrong with this picture?" Emma McCall muttered, as she plunged her hands into a mound of croissant dough. "It's pitch-black outside and I'm up to my elbows in flour."

Emma was the sole proprietor of The Scottish Captain, a bed-and-breakfast in Glory, North Carolina. Some days, though, the Captain seemed to own her. Today was a perfect example. She had risen at 4:00 a.m. because Calvin Constable, her breakfast chef, had taken a well-earned day off. That left Emma on her own to prepare this morning's breakfast, until Peggy Lyons, her housekeeper, arrived at six.

Emma glanced at the wall clock in the kitchen. Ten to six. If Peggy came on time—and if nothing went wrong—they would finish with ten minutes to spare. Just enough time to strip off her scruffy T-shirt and faded blue jeans and slip into one of her chic hostess outfits. Today she might go for the tailored suit in a shade of tan that went well with her dark brown hair.

The Captain had six guest rooms and could accommodate a maximum of eighteen guests in a pinch, although off-season bookings rarely exceeded half a dozen. On this, the first Wednesday in November, Emma had to prepare breakfast for five people.

The centerpiece dish would be Eggs Sardou, a classic New Orleans concoction of poached eggs served on artichokes with spinach and hollandaise sauce. She would also offer a selection of imported bacon and sausages, hot croissants, fresh-squeezed orange juice and her "signature" gingered fruit compote. And, of course, coffee and brewed tea.

Emma had decided to serve an elaborate breakfast because three of her guests were New England travel writers, part of a contingent on a pre-winter junket through North Carolina. Their favorable recommendations might bring flocks of northern "snowbirds" to The Scottish Captain as they traveled south. The other two guests—a couple who hailed from Maryland—also had influence. He was a prominent Washington attorney, she an evening news anchor on a Baltimore TV station.

Emma had just begun to shape croissants on a large buttered pan when Peggy Lyons burst into the kitchen and shouted, "There's a bug on the porch."

Emma willed herself not to scream at Peggy. She had seen this same panic-stricken look on her housekeeper's face many times before. Peggy was a fine worker but easily flustered by minor problems. Emma unstuck her fingers from the slick, buttery dough.

"Tromp on the bug, Peggy," she said, evenly. "Whap it with a newspaper, spray it with insecticide, or catch it in a jar. Pick one of the above, but do it quickly. I need your help."

"You don't understand, Emma. There's a *Bug* on the porch. A car! A silver Volkswagen Beetle convertible."

* * *

Rafe Neilson fumbled for his cell phone in the dark. He knew without looking at the glowing Caller ID display that Angie Ringgold needed his advice. Angie— a newcomer to the department—was the only police officer on duty in Glory, North Carolina, that morning.

"Good morning, Angie," he said sleepily.

"I'm sorry to call so early, Rafe, but someone pulled a weird prank on Broad Street. There's a Volkswagen Beetle sitting on The Scottish Captain's front porch."

"A prank?" He cleared his throat. "When did it become a police matter?"

"The Captain's owner dialed 911. She wants the responsible party arrested and I don't know what to tell her. Is moving a car to a porch a crime? And, if so, what kind of crime? The curriculum at the Police Academy stopped short of practical jokes."

Rafe peered at his clock—6:20 a.m. "Do you know who did the deed?"

"Sort of—but not exactly."

"What does 'sort of' mean?"

"There was a note tucked under the windshield wiper. I'll read it to you. 'Dear Emma. Your lack of support for enhancing the contemporary service really bugs us. Please reconsider your position.' The note is signed 'The Phantom Avenger.'"

Rafe thought about the message for a moment then groaned softly.

"See what I mean?" Angie said. "Sort of—but not exactly."

"I'll be there in three minutes."

Rafe slipped into his khaki trousers, tugged on a

warm sweatshirt and grabbed his nylon windbreaker. He'd worry about his police uniform later.

Outside, he fired up his Corvette—taking a moment to enjoy its throaty exhaust growl. Rafe's 'Vette was a 1978 model, candy-apple-red, a classic that he had lovingly restored and now kept in perfect operating condition.

Rafe's house on Front Street was five blocks from The Scottish Captain. He kept the 'Vette in second gear for the short drive. He parked across the street and took a moment to contemplate the front of the Captain in the flattering light of an unclouded sunrise.

Rafe chuckled to himself. The silver new Beetle looked at home up on the porch; passersby on Broad Street might well conclude that the bed-and-breakfast was also an eccentric automobile dealership.

The Captain was a large, three story clapboard structure, with a deep front lawn and a charming antique brick walkway. Every tourist guide to Glory explained that the old pile was considered one of the town's historical buildings. It had been built toward the end of the nineteenth century as an elegant residence for affluent single women. It was a good-looking house, with large windows, double front doors made of oak and a front porch served by a flight of five deep steps nearly twenty feet wide. The porch could hold a dozen chairs and sliders; it was the perfect sort of porch to cradle a compact convertible.

Rafe knew that the Captain had been a bed-and-breakfast since 1982. Before that, the building had served as Glory's cheapest rooming house, catering mostly to retired pensioners. Rafe recalled that Emma McCall, the current owner, had bought the Captain from Carole and Duncan Frasier, a pair of expatriate New Englanders. The Frasiers had picked up the aging residence for a song in 1981, renovated it into a B and B, and chose the name "The Scottish Captain" on the theory that it communicated three virtues: thrift, competence and a touch of wanderlust.

Rafe had toured the Captain two Christmases ago during an "open house afternoon" to raise money for the Glory Regional Hospital. He remembered that the first floor had both front and rear parlors, a dining room that had become the B and B's breakfast room, a kitchen and an ornate staircase that began in a high-ceilinged entrance foyer. There were six bedrooms of equal size on the second floor—three on each side of the hallway, each equipped with an en suite bathroom, not a common feature in the nineteenth century.

The tour didn't include the top story, but the docent explained that the third floor was a self-contained apartment—the owner's residence—accessible by a private staircase.

Rafe found Angie in her cruiser, writing in a notebook.

"Hi, Angie. Any progress?"

She nodded. "I've tentatively labeled the offense a 'Trespass.' Does that sound right to you?"

"Only if we want to consider a prank as a crime."

"The B and B owner is furious. As I told you, she wants to file a formal complaint."

"A natural first reaction. I'll try to change her mind."

Angie looked up from her writing. "That's right—you know Emma McCall."

Rafe grinned. "Sort of, but not exactly." He went on, "Where is she?"

"Working in the kitchen, at the rear of the building. That's why she didn't see or hear the Beetle lifted onto the porch."

"Do we know when it happened?"

"Well, I drove down Broad Street a few minutes after five and the car wasn't on the porch then."

"I'd better chat with the lady."

Rafe slapped the empty pockets of his windbreaker then offered an embarrassed smile. "I forgot my notebook. Can I borrow yours?"

"Sure. You can even keep my notes—if you promise to write up the official incident report."

"Consider it done. Can you also lend me a pen?"

"You need a wife to keep you organized," Angie said wryly.

"I'll take it under advisement."

Rafe walked along a narrow flagstone path to reach the back of The Scottish Captain. The top panes of the kitchen windows were open; the bottom were shuttered. He couldn't see inside, but whatever Emma McCall was cooking smelled wonderful.

He stopped to read Angie's notes.

Time of arrival on scene: 6:03 a.m.; Complainant: Emma McCall; female; Age: 37; Address: 18 Broad Street, Glory; Marital status: divorced; Hair: dark brown; Eyes: brown; Height: approx 5'9"; Occupation: innkeeper; Demeanor: angry; Weather: partly cloudy, cold; Nature of "trespass": vehicle moved from parking lot to porch of bed-and-breakfast; Estimated time of "trespass": between 5 and 6:00 a.m.; no apparent damage to B and B; no apparent damage to vehicle; Vehicle details: 2006 Volkswagen New Beetle convertible, silver, tan leather upholstery; Maryland registration: AM70RG3; Vehicle regis-

tered to Noelle R. Laurence, Catonsville, MD;
Vehicle not listed in National Crime Computer
System—presumably not stolen.

Rafe felt like laughing at the meticulous detail.
Rookie cops followed procedure to the letter and wrote
everything down.

One fact surprised him. He had guessed that
Emma—tall, graceful, good looking—was in her
early thirties. Because she was also a member of the
Glory Community Church Choir, he stood a few feet
away from her on most Wednesday evenings and
Sunday mornings. She seemed an odd duck, a loner
who relished her privacy. He had exchanged a few
pleasantries with her, but they had never shared a real
conversation.

The little he knew about Emma he'd picked up in
brief conversations with other choir members. She'd
moved to Glory about a year earlier from Seattle, Washington. Apparently, she'd held an important job at a
fancy hotel in Seattle but then decided she'd rather run
her own B and B.

Rafe knocked on the Captain's back door.

"Who's there?" asked a voice deep inside the kitchen.

"Rafe Neilson."

A hesitation. "Rafe Neilson from the *choir?*"

"The same—but today I'm Rafe Neilson from the
police."

Another hesitation. "Hang on."

Emma's face appeared at the window in the door. She
peered at him for a moment then opened the door halfway.

"I didn't know you were a policeman."

"My identification card is at home with my badge

and my wallet. You'll have to accept my word that I'm the deputy chief."

She opened the door fully. He stepped inside the kitchen.

"Let's say I believe you," she said. "Now what?"

"I need to talk with you about the report you made to Officer Ringgold."

She shook her head. "Sorry, I can't spare a moment right now. My guests expect to be served breakfast beginning at seven-thirty. It's twenty to seven and my housekeeper is setting up the dining room, which means that I have forty minutes to finish ten chores *and* change my clothes. Come back in two hours."

Rafe felt a twinge of sympathy for Emma. She was liberally dusted in flour that had settled beyond the borders of the large chef's apron she wore. She looked as frazzled as she sounded.

"What if I help you prepare breakfast?" he said. "We can talk while we work together."

"Do you know the difference between boysenberry conserve and boysenberry preserves?"

"I have to admit that I don't."

"Then come back in two hours. I don't let amateurs work in my kitchen."

Before Rafe could respond, the cell phone clipped to Emma's belt beeped.

"It's about time he returned my call," she murmured angrily as she flipped the phone open. "This is Emma."

Rafe listened intently to her half of the conversation. She didn't seem to object.

"Good morning, Mr. Yeager. Thanks for getting back to me so *quickly*....

"Yes, Peggy Lyons explained that she's your niece....

"I agree—she's a doll...."

"That's precisely what I said to the police—not all practical jokes are funny...."

"No—it weighs less than that. I looked up the weight of the Beetle on the Internet. The convertible is about three thousand pounds. Your whole team working together should have no problem...."

"Uh-huh... That's why I contacted you. Peggy tells me that you coach twenty-five of the strongest young men in the county...."

"Sure! The deal I propose is simple. I want that car off my porch as soon as possible. If your men help me this morning, I'll donate two couples' getaway weekends at the Captain that you can auction off to raise money for the team...."

"*Three* weekends?

"I understand—it's a worthy cause. But three weekends represents an enormous sum...."

"Very well—three weekends...."

"We'll be ready when you are...."

"Fine. I'll expect you in twenty minutes!"

Rafe swallowed a grin. Tom Yeager was a tough man to best in a bargain. Emma hooked the phone on her belt; she made no effort to hide her annoyance. "Do I have to explain the expensive negotiation you just overheard?" she asked.

"You rented our high school football team at a cost of three complimentary weekends."

"Whoever pulled this stunt cost me a small fortune. I'd sure love to see the perpetrators in handcuffs by the end of the day."

"You just hired the...*ah*...*perpetrators* to move the car off the porch."

"I *what?*"

"This is a small town. We don't have multiple collections of guys who are strong enough—and foolish enough—to tote a Volkswagen around."

"Rats! Why didn't I think of that before I made the deal?"

"The Glory Gremlins start football practice at 6:00 a.m. on Wednesday mornings. If some of them were inclined to move a car…"

"The team could do it on the way to the high school." Emma looked at Rafe with a confused frown. "But why me? I've never done anything to them."

"You read the note. Several of those kids are members of Glory Community Church."

"I read it, but it made no sense. I have absolutely nothing to do with the contemporary service at church."

Rafe tried not to show the astonishment he felt. Did Emma live in an isolation bubble? Her very lack of involvement with the contemporary service made her a target. Emma had been a member of the church for nearly a year. How could she be so oblivious to the ongoing turmoil at Glory Community?

A toilet flushed somewhere overhead. Emma jumped. "Oh, boy! My guests are getting up. I have to finish breakfast. Get out of my kitchen. *Now!*"

Rafe chose not to argue. He left without further comment and retraced the flagstone path to the front of the Captain, where a tall, big-bellied man in a blue, hooded sweatshirt was standing on the front lawn gazing up at the silver Beetle. His carefully trimmed gray beard made a perfect frame for the delighted smile on his face. As Rafe approached, the man said, "Tradition is a beautiful thing. I helped pull the same stunt forty years ago at the University of Maine. Of course, Volkswagen cars were smaller back then. We needed only a dozen seniors to carry a black Beetle to the chancellor's terrace. He…was…*frosted!*"

"Are you a guest at The Scottish Captain?" Rafe asked.

The man nodded. "The North Carolina Department of Tourism is shuttling a dozen travel writers around the state. Three of us are at the Captain, but I'm the only early riser. I was going for a prebreakfast walk around Glory, but a levitated Volkswagen seems so much more interesting. I wonder if we're witnessing the start of a new trend—the rediscovery of a decades-old practical joke?"

"Did you happen to see who did it?"

The man's smile didn't waver. "Elves. A giant flock of wee Scottish elves. Or possibly wood sprites. It's so hard to tell the difference—Officer."

"Is it that obvious?"

"The black notebook clutched in your hand gave you away. I used to cover the rural police beat for the *Daily Herald* in Portland, Maine. Small-town cops look alike."

Rafe returned to his Corvette to warm up. He was in a perfect position to observe the festivities fifteen minutes later.

The Glory Gremlins marched five abreast down the center of Broad Street in their gold-and-white practice uniforms, proudly led by the coaching staff.

To Rafe's surprise, Emma McCall and Peggy Lyons met the arriving team on the porch with two large trays of steaming paper cups. He guessed they were filled with hot chocolate. Apparently, Emma's earlier anger at the team had not overpowered her spirit of hospitality.

The football players downed the drinks and took up positions on either side of the Beetle.

Coach Yeager, serving both as cheerleader and lift master, shouted directions with many flourishes of his arms.

The Beetle rose and, like a glistening apparition, glided down the Captain's front steps, traversed the lawn and moved toward the small parking lot on the left side of the bed-and-breakfast. Emma McCall followed a few steps behind, arms crossed, jaw jutting. She now wore a dressy skirt and jacket that made Rafe think of a flight attendant's uniform. She looked cold and unhappy.

The silver car settled gently into a parking space, amidst a barrage of shouts and applause loud enough to wake every late sleeper on Broad Street.

Through it all, three enthusiastic picture-takers zigged and zagged around the young men. Rafe recognized one as Troy Huff, a local freelance photographer who often worked for the *Glory Gazette*. The second was the travel writer in the blue sweatshirt. The third was a striking blonde in a full-length shearling coat who brandished a palm-sized video camera. He guessed she was Noelle Laurence, the owner of the Volkswagen. The wide grin on her face signaled that she was having a grand old time. No way would she insist that someone be arrested.

What's left to talk about with Emma McCall?

Rafe decided to forgo his chat with the Captain's owner. Maybe she'd forget about filing a formal complaint. If not, she could come to police headquarters and cool her heels awhile outside his office.

Rafe started his Corvette and shifted to first gear. "In any case," he said to the steering wheel, "I'll see her this evening at choir practice."

He let out the clutch, wondering if he should tell Emma that the flour-spotted T-shirt she wore while cooking was actually more becoming than her mud-colored suit.

TWO

The silence pouring through the curtained windows of his study surprised Reverend Daniel Hartman. Anyone within two blocks of Glory Community Church on a Wednesday evening inevitably heard the choir practicing—and the manse was scarcely a hundred feet away. He rolled his swivel chair across the parquet floor to the window that overlooked the church. The lights were on in the choir practice room and he could see shadows of people moving inside. But where was Lily Kirk's piercing soprano voice? Or Tony Taylor's booming baritone? Daniel hadn't heard either for at least five minutes.

He glanced at his wristwatch. Ten minutes past seven. *Much too early for the choir to take a break.* Nina McEwen *always* demanded a solid half hour of practice between seven and seven-thirty. Nina was a tough taskmaster and a woman of unwavering habits: she enforced rules as if they were divine commandments.

"Something's not kosher," Daniel murmured as he saved the half-completed draft of the sermon he was writing and switched his laptop to "sleep" mode.

Daniel knew, of course, that giving in to his curiosity

was nothing but a convenient excuse for procrastination—but even a feeble pretext was better than none. For some reason, his message on John, Chapter eight was not "clicking." Better to set it aside until he felt moved by authentic inspiration. Perhaps the Holy Spirit preferred a different text on Sunday.

You were going to stop sermonizing soon, anyway.

The Reverend Doctor Daniel Hartman, Minister of Word and Sacrament, had a standing appointment with Nina McEwen, Doctor of Fine Arts, Glory Community's Choral Director. They met every Wednesday, immediately after choir practice, to select the hymns that would be sung a week from the coming Sunday.

Nina preferred that Daniel not attend the actual rehearsal itself. "I need to be top dog in the room when we practice," Nina once explained. "The choir has to know that my word is their law."

Daniel had spent more than twenty years as a U.S. Army chaplain and understood the principle of "chain of command." If Nina felt that the pastor's presence might undercut the authority the choirmaster needed—well, he would schedule his arrival after the last Amen was sung.

He peered again at the choir practice room window. Had that happened yet tonight?

There's only one way to find out.

A plump raindrop thumped against the windshield just as Emma drove her Volvo station wagon past the brightly lit sign at the start of Main Street that proclaimed in six-inch-high, gold-and-red letters: Welcome To Glory, North Carolina. We're Happy You're Here!

"Not half as happy as I am," Emma muttered tiredly.

A routine ninety-minute drive from Portsmouth,

Virginia, had become a two-and-a-half-hour creep through lashing rain, with the windshield wipers on the Volvo straining on high for much of the trip. Now the on-again, off-again rainstorm looked ready to start up again during the evening.

The traffic light at the corner of Main Street and King turned red. Emma wished that she had visited the advertising agency that morning, as planned, rather than letting it slip to the afternoon.

That stupid prank upset my day.

Breakfast at the Captain had turned into a festive celebration, with Noelle Laurence, the Baltimore newscaster who happened to own the Beetle, arranging impromptu interviews with Emma and Coach Yeager.

"I hope my homemade videotape is usable," she said. "I'd love to run this story on the *Five O'Clock News.*"

Emma couldn't imagine why anyone in Baltimore would care about a Volkswagen on her porch. She was even a bit surprised when Rex Grainger, the editor of the *Glory Gazette,* called to verify the name of the car's owner. Friday's issue, he promised, would include a hard-hitting exposé entitled "The Beetle Battle: Glory Gremlins 1, Vandals 0."

He wasted ten valuable minutes commiserating with me about my wasted morning.

Everything Emma had done that day took longer than usual. Cleaning up after breakfast, checking guests out, confirming reservations, helping Peggy Lyons prepare the bedrooms—they all dragged on past their allotted times. Emma finally left for Portsmouth at one o'clock and spent longer than she meant to chatting with Todd Harris at the agency.

You should have declined that last cup of coffee,
Emma thought, guiltily.

Giving in had seemed the friendly thing to do. Todd
was in a chatty mood as he presented the new designs for
her brochures, Web site and menu covers. He wanted to
talk about strategies for marketing The Scottish Captain
to vacationers from Great Britain. He suggested another
cup of coffee, and Emma forgot about the threatening sky
and her intention to go to choir practice that evening.

Glory Community Church had a fine, but small, choir.
As Nina McEwen, the choral director, often said, "With
only seventeen singers, every voice counts." Emma tried
her best not to miss church services or practice sessions.

The traffic light turned green; Emma turned left onto
King Street. It was now raining quite heavily. She
looked at the dashboard clock. Ten after seven.

I'll only be a little late.

There was no other traffic in sight as she drove three
blocks north then made a right turn into Glory Community's parking lot.

She stepped out of the dark red Volvo and almost
collided with Reverend Daniel Hartman.

"Good evening, Emma," he said, as he pirouetted out
of her path.

"Oh! I didn't see you."

"Let's get out of the rain." He tugged open the back
door.

Emma walked into a cacophony of heated words.
The raised voices filling the corridor were angry—and
easy for her to recognize.

"Nonsense!" Lily Kirk bellowed. "Your bad
behavior has nothing to do with worship. The young

people in this church are ungrateful whelps, with no appreciation for tradition."

"Nobody says 'whelp' anymore," Debbie shouted back. "You talk like you think—out of date."

"Oh, my!" Daniel said. "Our star sopranos are dueling." He scooted around Emma and plunged into the practice room. She halted in the doorway and watched the fracas unfold.

Lily and Debbie stood on opposite sides of Nina, who kept whacking her music stand with her conductor's baton.

"Where is the respect that *my* generation showed its elders?" Lily ranted. "We never would have stooped to committing spiteful practical jokes. Imagine tormenting a defenseless fish!"

"If you want respect from me, earn it!" Debbie returned heatedly. "And for your information, we don't do practical jokes. Because you have the media on your side, we've been forced to launch a campaign of harmless civil disobedience to get our position better known. The fish, by the way, seemed happier in his new home."

Nina whacked harder, flinging specks of white paint in all directions.

Reverend Hartman tried to intervene. "Please, ladies! Please! This is neither the time nor place to argue about church business."

The sixtyish Lily, who had once sung on Broadway, ignored both pastor and director and upped the stakes. She spread her arms wide and belted out, "Spiteful! Spiteful! Spiteful!" Each crystal-clear word pitched higher than the one before.

Debbie, a seventeen-year-old high school student, couldn't match Lily's colossal volume, but she did manage to hit an even more shrill high note when she sang, "Out of date! Out of date! Out of date!"

Nina smashed her baton against the music stand in a mighty final whack that sent the baton's red tip flying over Emma's head and out the door.

"Nooo!" Nina shrieked. She flung her broken symbol of musical authority against the back wall. "This is *intolerable*. Fifteen-minute break!"

Emma stepped aside. Nina—hands trembling, tears in her eyes—ran past her and made for the ladies' room.

"*Now* see what you've done?" Lily leveled an accusing finger at Debbie, who seemed, Emma thought, to be genuinely dismayed by Nina's abrupt departure.

Before Debbie could reply, Tony Taylor, the choir's lead baritone, a retired naval officer who owned the Glory at Sea marina, entered the fray. "That's not fair, Lily! This is your doing. You started the ruckus by baiting Debbie—she merely defended herself."

Lily held her ground. "Of course *you* would take the girl's side. You *also* sing at the contemporary service." She hissed the word *contemporary* as if it was obscene.

"I agree with Lily!" said Lane Johnson, the choir's lead tenor and Glory's postmaster. He threw back his broad shoulders and glared at Tony. "You've never liked the traditional hymns—probably because you sing a weak baritone."

"Who asked for your dumb opinion?" Tony growled at Lane.

"Who made you king of the choir?" Lane barked back.

Emma wasn't sure whether Tony or Lane landed the first push, but a moment later the pair was wrestling on the floor, surrounded by fallen music stands and hymnals.

Rafe Neilson, who had been standing in the back

row with Sam Lange, the choir's other baritone, raced forward to pull Tony and Lane apart, while Jacqueline Naismith, a retired schoolteacher who sang alto, used her considerable bulk to shield a small, vulnerable table that held several pitchers of iced tea and a tray of cookies. The other members of the choir watched the spectacle with grim determination. Emma noted that some of them were actually *enjoying* the brawl.

BWANG!

The raucous noise made Emma spin around. She saw Daniel Hartman standing next to the piano and realized that he had slammed both hands down on the keyboard to end the fight. Rafe yanked Tony to his feet in one powerful heave and then reached back down for Lane.

"We will have an interlude of prayer!" Daniel roared, in a commanding voice that Emma concluded must have been perfected in the military.

All extraneous movement in the choir ceased. Heads bowed instantly. Emma lowered her chin to her chest but kept her eyes wide open.

"Lord," Daniel began, "we ask for Your peace tonight. There's a storm blowing through Glory Community and only You can help calm the waters. You know better than us that truly devoted believers often disagree about the best ways to advance the Kingdom of God. Well—give all of us the hearts to forgive our debtors. And help us to remember that we raise our voices in this building for one purpose only—to proclaim *Your* glory. In Jesus's name we pray."

Emma joined in the rumbling group "Amen." Daniel Hartman had spoken a fairly reasonable prayer—one she had no qualms affirming.

Daniel continued, "Someone find Nina. Assure her that her choir will be prepared to sing rather than fight after the break."

Emma felt a touch on her arm. She turned and saw Rafe's smiling face.

"You look confused," he said. "Don't you know what's going on at our church?"

Emma fought to control her irritation at his remark. She scanned the practice room. The choir had broken into several small groups. No one was looking their way. She bent her head close to his.

"If you had asked me this morning, Mr. Neilson, I would have gladly explained that I am *not* a member of Glory Community Church. I sing in your choir for three specific reasons. *One,* I have a good voice. *Two,* I enjoy choral singing. *And three,* Nina McEwen is a fabulous choral director.

"Moving right along—I understand all too well how churches work. The chief reason I chose not to join Glory Community Church is that The Scottish Captain keeps me busy fifteen hours a day and I have no time left for church politics or taking sides in silly debates. I had intended to join Glory Community, but Nina was kind enough to warn me about the current fight, without giving me any details. I decided to bide my time. I saw no need to become part of a church in crisis."

Emma was pleased to note that her declaration knocked the wind out of Rafe's sails. His smile had faded as she spoke, along with the grating *I'm-a-cop-who-knows-everything* self-assurance written across his face.

But along with her amusement, Emma felt a surprising stab of guilt. She had told Rafe the truth, but not the whole truth. The ongoing fight was only part of the reason she'd refused to become a member of Glory Community.

Two years earlier, Emma's then husband had filed for a no-fault divorce, moved out of their home and announced that he really, truly loved another woman. Much to Emma's astonishment, most of her church friends back in Seattle blamed her for the failure of the marriage.

"Emma put her career ahead of her marriage."

"Emma canceled too many vacations because of her work."

"Emma should have quit her job and had children like a normal woman."

Her small group, the people she worked with on the church's hospitality team, even the other members of the praise choir turned against her.

Emma drove the unhappy memories away by focusing on the present. "Perhaps I'll change my mind when the brawling is over," she said to Rafe.

"I assumed that everyone in the choir was also a member of the church," he said.

"Why would you assume that?"

He shook his head. He started to speak, but shook his head again and gazed into the distance.

Emma found herself intrigued by the way Rafe was suddenly tongue-tied. It gave him the demeanor of a little lost boy—and, surprisingly, made him seem attractive to Emma for the first time today.

She used the opportunity to study Rafe. He stood a bit over six feet tall and had the lithe, athletic frame of a man who frequently worked out at a gym. He had short sandy hair, deep-set hazel eyes and an agreeably handsome face—now that his earlier arrogance had vanished. Perhaps she could help him remove the foot he had placed so squarely in his mouth?

"This morning you seemed surprised that I didn't understand the Phantom Avenger's message to me. Please tell me what I need to know."

Rafe hesitated. Emma could almost hear him thinking, *Does she really mean it?* He eventually gave a cautious nod of agreement. "Have you heard of the Caruthers bequest?"

"Nary a word."

"John Caruthers was a choir member for thirty years. When he died last year, he left the church six hundred thousand dollars. John put one stipulation on his gift—it must be used to advance the church's ministry of music."

"How?"

"That's the root of the problem. Two groups have come up with plans for investing the bequest. One wants to replace our electronic organ with a full-size pipe organ to enhance the traditional service. The other wants to rebuild the sanctuary and install the kind of electronic instruments and audiovisual equipment to support a world-class contemporary service. The two schools of thought have hardened into opposite sides. The church is split down the middle."

Emma sighed heavily. "Why do so many Christians I meet fight with each other about church?"

"The fans of the contemporary service invented the Phantom Avenger. You heard Debbie Akers—she and her colleagues have launched their self-styled campaign of civil disobedience because the *Glory Gazette* has come out on the side of the Traditionalists." He peered inquiringly at her. "You have heard of the *Gazette?*"

"Of course. I spoke to the editor today. He seemed very sympathetic."

"Rex Grainger sang with Lily Kirk in the choir for more than two decades. He retired from the choir three years ago, but the *Gazette* is squarely in the Traditionalist camp."

"He promised to publish a hard-hitting story about the Beetle."

"Rex will need to add pages. The Phantom Avenger struck four times this week."

"More cars on porches?"

"In the middle of Monday morning, someone moved a two-foot-long koi fish from Richard Squires's pond to the Memorial Fountain opposite Town Hall."

"So that's the defenseless fish that Lily mentioned."

"The Phantom's note said, 'We won't *scale* down our demands for a better contemporary service."

Emma chuckled. "The Phantom has a bizarre sense of humor."

"Fortunately, our fountain is fed by unchlorinated springwater—or else that koi would be history. Richard claims his big goldfish is twenty-five years old and worth more than two thousand bucks."

Emma looked across the practice room at a balding man in his fifties who sang tenor in the choir. He was engaged in an animated conversation with Tony Taylor. She turned back to Rafe and said, "Richard must support the Traditionalists."

"All the way. He loves hymns and hates praise music." He chuckled. "And so does Lily Kirk. Yesterday, someone dressed up the statue of Moira McGregor in Founders Park to look like Lily and put a sign around her neck. 'Attention, all pigeons in the vicinity of Glory.

Please show Ms. Kirk what you think of the traditional service. The Phantom Avenger strikes again!'"

Emma tried not to laugh, but a giggle came out nonetheless. She quickly said, "Who was the target of the fourth prank?"

Rafe seemed to fight back a smile. "Gary Porter— my boss. Yesterday, Chief Porter found a phony parking ticket tied to his radio antenna. It read, 'Caught in the act of *trafficking* with blowhard Traditionalists who insist on buying an old-fashioned pipe organ. We believe that you would come to church regularly to worship at an *arresting* contemporary service. Don't *fail to yield!*'"

"Is the chief a member of the church?"

"No, but his daughter is. Michelle Porter Engle." Rafe gestured discreetly toward the petite redhead who stood chatting with Lily Kirk. "One of your fellow sopranos—and also a steadfast advocate of our traditional service."

Emma leaned back against the wall. She really wanted to sit down, but the only unoccupied chairs were across the room. "How did I get lumped in with the Traditionalists?"

Rafe shrugged. "Most of the choir supports the traditional service. That's the way I feel—and that's how I had you pegged. The Avenger must have made the same mistake."

"Do you know who the Phantom is?"

"I have my suspicions." He chuckled.

"Are you going to do anything about it?"

"If you mean, do I plan to arrest the ringleaders, the answer is no. You won't see any perps in handcuffs tonight."

"I didn't get my hopes up real high. I know how law enforcement works in small towns where everyone knows everyone else. I grew up in an even smaller town in northeastern Pennsylvania."

"It's not that simple. First, I haven't been able to determine what crimes were committed. We don't have a statute or ordinance that criminalizes the relocation of a big goldfish. Second, I don't see any criminal intent in what was done—the pranks are technical violations, at worst. However…" Rafe's expression became serious. "However, I plan to speak to the folks involved face-to-face and explain why you—and Richard Squires—are extremely displeased. I'll try to arrange some free yard work in return for your three complimentary weekends."

Emma took a moment to think about it. "That seems fair enough, considering no real damage was done. My porch is okay, and the couple from Baltimore drove north after breakfast. Case closed!" She peered at him. "Do cops really say that?"

"Sure. Except this case won't be really closed until our church decides how to spend the six hundred thousand dollars." Rafe looked down at his hands. "Paul was right—money *is* the root of all evil."

"He didn't write that." Emma waited until Rafe glanced quizzically at her. "Paul had nothing against wealth. He warned us against the *love of money.*"

"Are you sure?"

"Absolutely. Check out First Timothy. Chapter six. Near the middle."

"I'm impressed. You know your Bible." He offered a rueful smile. "I wish I did."

"I've been studying the Bible since I was a kid."

Rafe laughed. "A Bible whiz who refuses to join a church—that's an odd combination."

"Not really," Emma said quietly. "I love Christianity. It's those Christians that fight I can do without."

THREE

The blue clapboard Victorian on Front Street was a smaller house than Rafe had wanted. It had only one full bathroom and a single-car garage, and cost half-again more than he had planned to spend, thanks to its stunning view of Albemarle Sound. But his teenage daughter, Kate, had loved the "gingerbread-detailed charmer" from the instant she saw its picture pinned up in the front window of the Realtor's. That had been enough to sway Rafe.

Every light in the house was turned on when Rafe maneuvered his Corvette into the driveway—a gentle protest by Kate that he had left home before sunup and was returning fourteen hours later. A small-town policeman's lot included long days, but Rafe usually managed to eat breakfast and supper at home. Today, the pranks had gotten in the way.

He found her in the living room watching a cheerleading DVD. He moved behind her and kissed the top of her head just as a blond cheerleader on the TV screen tumbled to the ground from the top of a three-layer pyramid of fellow cheerleaders.

"Oooh, that's gotta hurt," Kate said.

"Is this some sort of training video? Teaching you about safety, I hope."

"Uh-uh. It's an hour of cheerleading goofs and bloopers. Funny stuff."

"Not for the gals who hit the ground hard. Or their parents." Rafe came around to the front of the sofa and sat down next to Kate. She was fifteen, with a tall, long-legged, athletic build and a face that was pretty and intelligent at the same time. She had big brown eyes, fine features and shoulder-length reddish-brown hair. Rafe's eyes flicked toward the framed photograph atop a bookcase. Kate was becoming more like her mother with every passing day.

"I'm on the freshman cheerleader squad, remember?" Kate said. "No jumps or stunts or pyramids."

"For which I am exceptionally grateful."

She used the remote to turn off the TV. "Anything interesting happen today?"

He grinned and tapped the end of her nose. "A good try, but I'm sure that every kid in town knows about the Volkswagen."

She countered by tapping his nose. "How was choir practice? Anything unusual happen?"

"Wow. You even know about the fight. I'm impressed—the power of cell phones in the hands of teenagers is awesome."

Rafe felt sure that she cracked a smile.

"I didn't arrest anyone tonight," he said, "but I will if there are any more wrestling matches at church. We actually had a pretty good rehearsal after the hotheads cooled down."

Kate nodded.

"My theory," he said, "is that the epidemic of pranks in Glory has put lots of people on edge."

Kate focused her eyes on the remote control in her lap.

"Let's go off the record," he said. "I want to send a message to the student who's planning the gags. I presume you know who's in charge, since you know everything about everyone under the age of twenty-one within a radius of fifty miles."

"Why assume a kid is responsible?"

"Because I don't know any adults who could convince the high school football team to move a Volkswagen Beetle from a parking lot to a porch."

"It's not that simple…." She finished the sentence with a shrug.

"No?"

"There isn't a single student in charge—it's more of a committee."

"Committees have chairpersons."

"This one has a book."

"A book…?"

"*Great Practical Jokes of the 1950s and 1960s.* It's an antique, published way back in 1970. Kids are passing it around Glory High like the baton in a relay race. Whoever has the book must do one of the jokes. Then he or she gives the book to someone else who has the nerve to do another one."

"Specifically, a high school student who also supports the contemporary service at Glory Community Church?"

"Well, *duh!*"

"Do you have to attend our church to receive the book?"

"Nope. You just have to know what kind of music you prefer."

"Do I have to ask which side you're on?"

"I think organ chords are icky. They make me think of old horror movies. Anyway, I like to hear drums when I listen to music, and they never have drums in a traditional service."

"Never?"

"Never!" She added a definitive shake of her head.

Rafe thought about it and realized that Kate might be right. He had seen many kinds of musical instruments played at traditional church services—violins, cellos, trumpets, guitars, flutes, trombones, pianos, bells, even an accordion—but never a full drum set. Those who favored drum-accompanied music would probably prefer a contemporary service. Of course, Kate also seemed to have more than a passing interest in the seventeen-year-old male drummer who played at Glory Community every Sunday.

"Tell me more about this antique book," he said.

"It's incredibly cool…" she began, and then realized her mistake.

"I get it. The book was passed to you."

"No comment."

"I assume that means you committed a prank."

Kate fiddled with the remote in her hands. "You'll never get me to confess to anything."

"Then let me play detective. You don't know much about cars, so you wouldn't come up with the idea of moving a Volkswagen. You're too smart—and I think too compassionate—to risk killing a fish. You don't have easy access to the old clothing placed on Moira McGregor. But you do have a fancy computer, several graphics programs and a good ink-jet printer. I think you created the phony traffic ticket found dangling from Chief

Porter's radio antenna. In fact, the more I think about it the more sense it makes. You weren't taking much risk marching into the parking lot behind Police Headquarters and affixing said ticket. If anyone spotted you, you could simply say you left something in my 'Vette."

"I admit to nothing."

"The clincher is the spelling error."

Kate peered at him quizzically.

"You wrote 'trafficing,' without the *k*. The correct spelling is trafficking. We both know that spelling is your weakest subject."

Kate pushed a lock of hair away from her face but said nothing. Rafe pressed on. "Where did the book come from? Don't try to tell me it's on loan from the school library."

"Well, I don't know this for a total fact, but I think the book came from Sam Lange's bookstore."

Rafe grunted. The Glory Book Nook was the logical source for an "antique" book. Although Sam sold both new and used books, he seemed to make more money from the old volumes on his shelves. He specialized in quirky topics and did a thriving Internet business with book collectors.

"Okay, I'll do some more detecting. Jake Moore, a junior at Glory High, works three afternoons a week and all day Saturday at the Book Nook, so he had the means to acquire the book in question. Jake is also a member of the church choir, which gives him a motive...*except*..."

"Except what?"

"Jake doesn't like the contemporary service. He's supposed to be on the same side as Lily Kirk. So he can't be involved."

"Right."

"Except…"

"Now what?"

"That 'right' you just spoke sounded suspicious. It's got me thinking."

"About what?"

"About how devilishly clever your side is." He poked at her ribs. "Jake Moore is an undercover agent. You placed a spy in the opposition's camp."

"I have no idea what you are talking about," she said airily.

"Okay, then let's talk about the book some more. How nasty do the collected pranks get?"

"Well, the book shows you how to do lots of things that go 'bang.' A couple of guys were interested, but these days you can't go to a drugstore and buy the ingredients to make homemade explosives."

"And the people said, 'Amen!'"

"Some of the pranks are impossibly gross. Itching powder, stink bombs and paper bags filled with horse manure."

"I know that one! You put the paper bag on the victim's porch, set fire to the top of the bag and ring the bell. Most people put out the fire by stomping on the bag."

Kate grimaced. "That's *awful*. I don't like jokes that need to be cleaned up with a shovel. Pranks should make people laugh."

"Like a phony parking ticket presented to the chief of police?"

"That sounds funny to me."

"Actually, the Chief wasn't amused in any way, shape or form. He offered to shoot the person responsible."

Kate sat up straight. "Are we finished talking about practical jokes?"

"Do you have another topic in mind?"

"I've been told that you were checking out Emma McCall this morning at The Scottish Captain."

"Checking her out?"

"Watching her with more than professional interest."

"Who told you that?"

"You were also seen talking with her tonight at church."

Rafe felt his eyebrows rise. Who, he wondered, was Kate's source of information? He tried to remember if Jake Moore was also a member of the Glory Gremlins. He was certainly large enough to play football.

"And your point is?" Rafe said.

"You are considered absolutely awesome, while everyone knows that she's a total loser. Think carefully before you do anything that might ruin your reputation."

Rafe didn't want to laugh aloud, but he couldn't stop himself.

"The poppers are magnificent here," Lily said, "I recommend them highly. I believe they're homemade."

Emma knew better. Dan's Pizza Deluxe undoubtedly bought frozen, machine-made poppers, ten-pounds at a time, but why shatter Lily's illusions or begin a pointless discussion about the tawdry secrets of cheap restaurants?

Emma scanned the menu quickly. It seemed late for deep-fried jalapeño peppers stuffed with cream cheese, but a greasy pizza might be even less digestible. And more expensive. She guessed that Lily was stretching a tight budget to pay for their impromptu after-rehearsal snack.

"Why don't we share an order of poppers?" Emma said.

"That's a grand idea." Lily sounded relieved as she caught the waitress's attention. "One order of poppers and two iced teas."

Emma waited patiently for Lily to begin the conversation—almost certainly a long-winded recruiting speech encouraging Emma to become active in the ongoing church battle. Why couldn't people understand that she didn't care enough about the issue to take sides? Why couldn't they simply leave her alone?

Emma had been walking to her Volvo when Lily suddenly appeared at her side. "We don't know each other very well, Mrs. McCall, but I have a question that I must ask you."

Emma didn't point out that McCall was her maiden name and she had abandoned the "Mrs." label when she moved to Glory. She simply said, "A question? About what?"

"The rain may begin again at any minute. Why don't we go for quick snack? My treat, of course." Lily gestured toward an old Ford Taurus sedan.

Reluctantly, Emma dropped her car keys into her purse. She had been awake since four-thirty and wanted to get to bed, but Lily possessed a peculiar authority—a strange presence—that compelled Emma to agree. She obediently followed the woman to the well-cared-for silver Ford and opened the passenger's door. She paid little attention to the elderly vehicle until she slid past the high side bolsters on her bucket seat.

This feels like a sports car seat.

Emma looked around. Enough light spilled into the car from the lampposts in the church's parking lot to see that the Taurus had black-leather interior and a five-

Glory Be!

speed manual transmission. Lily pushed the clutch pedal and worked the ignition key. The engine roared to life and settled into a thrumming idle.

Lily revved the engine and turned to Emma. "This is my baby, my one luxury. She's a Taurus SHO, one of the first built in 1989. 'SHO' stands for super high output. There's a three-liter Yamaha V6 under the hood. Top speed is supposed to be 143 miles per hour, but I've never had her above 120."

Emma pulled her seat belt tight as Lily accelerated along King Street.

"I enjoy life in the fast lane," Lily said, with a giggle, as she accelerated again. "But only at night when most of the cops in town are asleep." She braked hard, downshifted and then made a screeching right turn onto Main Street.

Emma watched the dark road whiz past. Beyond Glory's town limits, Main Street became State Route 34A, which ran north to Route 17 then on to Elizabeth City, some twenty miles away. Dan's Pizza Deluxe was about a mile up the road. Halfway there, Lily tooted her car's horn.

"What's that for?" Emma had asked.

"I like to give the animals a fair warning," Lily had said. "A honk now and then gives the raccoons and deer a chance to get out of our way." Lily patted Emma's hand. "You won't tell anybody, will you?"

"Tell them what?"

"About my speeding and horn blowing." Lily had laughed. "It's my little secret. Only a few of my friends know. Most people in Glory think I'm a mild-mannered retired librarian who never drives faster than fifty-five miles per hour."

Emma joined in the laughter. "Your little secret is safe with me."

The waitress brought their drinks. She was a slender young woman with dyed red hair and a sour expression that Emma doubted did much to encourage food sales. "Your poppers will be out in a minute."

Lily waited until they were alone before she said, "I appreciate your willingness to take time away from The Scottish Captain to meet with me. I've been told that innkeepers are on duty twenty-four hours a day."

"Well, some days are longer than others," Emma replied.

This one, for example.

Lily pressed on, "I've never stayed at a bed-and-breakfast, so I can only guess how much work is involved. Do your guests expect you to be on call throughout the day?"

Emma tried to read Lily's face. She seemed genuinely interested in the mechanics of running a B and B.

"I try to be available when guests are up and about. My housekeeper holds down the fort two or three afternoons a week so that I can run errands. Today, for example, I had an appointment in Norfolk. Tomorrow, I have to drive to Elizabeth City to interview a new food supplier."

"Ah." Lily's face brightened. "Then it is likely I will see you again tomorrow evening."

"Tomorrow evening?" Emma felt bewildered by Lily's sudden change of tack.

"I'll be a guest at the next meeting of the Writing for Glory Club."

"Now I understand," Emma said. The local writer's club, chaired by Sara Knoll met twice a month—the first and third Thursdays—at The Scottish Captain. "Are you a writer?"

"Oh, no. Sara Knoll invited me to hear her talk about her work in progress. We've become good friends during the past few months. She's been exceptionally generous with her computer expertise." Lily peered at Emma. "You do know that Ms. Knoll has authored more than a dozen published books."

"Of course." Everyone who attended Glory Community Church knew that Sara wrote the popular *Martha Does It* series of how-to books for women on subjects that ranged from household hints to electrical wiring to setting up a computer network. "Come a few minutes early and browse around the Captain. I'm proud of the renovations and redecorating I've done."

"Renovations?" Lily said sharply. "Have you done any major reconstruction?"

"Our kitchen is new and so are the guest bathrooms. The six guest bedrooms have new wallpaper and carpeting."

"Did you make any structural changes to the first floor?"

"Nothing significant. Do you know the Captain?"

"It's been many years since I've been inside." Lily stared into space for several seconds. "I may accept your kind offer to browse around—assuming of course that I survive those miserable pranksters."

Emma took a sip of iced tea.

Here it comes. A sales pitch to join her "side."

But Lily surprised Emma. She, too, began to sip her tea and said nothing more until the waitress arrived with a platter of poppers and two smaller plates.

"They look especially good tonight." Lily slid a popper onto her plate. "I hope you enjoy them."

The poppers provided a second surprise for Emma.

They were baked rather than fried and didn't look mass-produced. She sliced one into thirds and tasted a piece.

"These are superb," she said. "They *are* homemade."

"Dave is an extraordinary cook. He used to be the hors d'oeuvre chef at the Hamilton House Hotel in New York City. He's *another* big-city native who moved to Glory."

Emma felt mildly annoyed at the way Lily emphasized "another." She responded with, "I believe you wanted to ask me a question."

Lily flushed slightly. "Yes, although I've been doing my best to avoid it." She sighed. "I'd best dive right in. I couldn't help notice you speaking with Rafe Neilson at the church this evening. Did you by any chance discuss the wave of pranks sweeping Glory?"

"Among other things," Emma said, in a harsher tone than she meant to.

Lily's expression grew tense. "I'm not trying to pry into your personal relationships, Mrs. McCall. I have a reason for asking."

Emma paused to regain her composure. "We did talk about the pranks. A total of four have been committed. I became the…*subject* of the fourth practical joke this morning."

"So I heard. The ancient 'Beetle on the porch' gag." Lily carefully set her knife and fork down on her plate. "Does he know whether any of the mischief was mean-spirited? Does the so-called 'Phantom Avenger' wish to cause physical harm to his victims?"

"The four pranks were silly attacks on property, not people." Emma abruptly pictured a flock of pigeons settling on the *real* Lily Kirk. She swallowed a snigger. "Rafe doesn't see any criminal intent in what was done."

"He told you that?"

"Those are his words."

Lily nodded slowly. "That makes me feel much better. You see, earlier this evening a pickup truck nearly pushed me off the road."

"My goodness!" Emma set her own fork down. "When? Where?"

"Two miles north on State Route 34A. About a quarter to seven. I'd driven to an industrial supply shop in Elizabeth City to buy a tube of the glue I use to repair books and I was racing through the rain to be on time for choir practice." Lily hesitated, as if she were reluctant to relive the memory.

"Go on." Emma thought back to earlier that evening. At a quarter to seven she'd been on the same road, but had been farther away from town.

"All at once I saw a huge grill in my rearview mirror. The truck actually tapped me—you can see the dent in the back bumper. I tromped on the gas and got out of there. I didn't see the truck after that."

"Do you think the driver hit you on purpose?"

"My first thought was that a prankster was trying to frighten me. But it may have been nothing more than an exuberant teenager who got careless while driving his father's pickup truck."

"Did you tell the police?"

"I intended to talk to Rafe after choir practice. But now I don't dare bother him—not after the *contretemps* at church this evening."

Emma needed a moment to remember that *contretemps* meant quarrel. "A quarrel in the choir is one thing. But if someone tried to harm you...I think you should talk to Rafe. He seems reasonable."

"Most women in Glory find him more than reason-able," Lily smiled. "We don't have an abundance of thirty-eight-year-old, good-looking single men in Glory." She shook her head. "No. This time I won't talk to Rafe. A dent in my back bumper doesn't prove any-thing. And since the pranks are essentially harmless, Rafe is likely to conclude I'm a hysterical older woman who suffers from a touch of paranoia."

Emma chewed on a piece of popper and made a mental note to talk to Dave about providing poppers—and other appetizers—to the Scottish Captain. She also wondered what she should do about the fear she heard in Lily's voice.

FOUR

Daniel Hartman peered into the church's refrigerator and allowed himself to sigh. "No real cream, and no milk," he said. "All I can offer you is powdered creamer."

"That will do me fine," Sara Knoll replied. "After twenty-five years as an international journalist, I'm used to tight rations and impromptu meeting places."

"In that event, let's talk right here. What could be more impromptu than our kitchen?" He handed her a ceramic mug full of coffee and gestured toward a pair of wooden stools next to a stainless-steel food preparation table. "I don't want to keep you long tonight, but I do want to review the progress your committee is making."

Daniel sipped his own coffee. The church's Elder Board had appointed a committee to recommend how to spend the Caruthers bequest. Sara was its chair—an excellent choice, given her background and experience. Daniel considered Sara a no-nonsense, get-the-job-done professional. She would have made a fine army officer had she chosen a different career path.

"What progress?" She shrugged. "We're deadlocked."

"How can you be? You have five members. That means no tie votes."

She smiled wryly. "We agreed from the start to require a minimum of four votes to make a final recommendation. Alas, our committee consists of two inflexible Contemporaries, two unyielding Traditionalists, and me. I abstain whenever we vote because that's the only way I know to stay friendly with both sides."

"Has it worked?

"So far." Sara added a nod. "I'm perceived as neutral—which has helped both sides to remain civil to each other during our meetings." A frown spread across her face. "But our civility hasn't translated into progress. I can summarize what the committee has done with a single word—*nothing*."

Daniel paused to gather his thoughts. "I fear for the future of Glory Community Church. Our highly polarized rift is the kind of conflict that can wreck a church fellowship. What bothers me most is that I don't know how to get our people to back down from their sincerely held positions." He added, "The elders rightly expect me to get everyone working toward a solution that will make the whole congregation happy."

"Isn't that a trick that pastors learn on the job?" she said with another smile.

He grinned back. "I spent twenty-one years in the U.S. Army and rose through the ranks to become a colonel, commanding a cadre of other chaplains. My experience taught me leadership, not conflict resolution."

"I presume that shouting 'Attention!' has a greater effect in the army than in a church."

"Oh, I can yell loud enough to stop a fight in the choir loft, but what do I do next? I wish that your

'Martha' books included a volume on compromise and forgiveness." He toasted Sara with his coffee mug. "Your new book on working with stained glass will come in handy should we have to replace broken panels in the sanctuary."

"Sorry, but *Stained Glass Made Simple* is the *next* book in the series. The one I have to deliver the day before Thanksgiving is called *Finding Undiscovered Treasures in Your Attic.*"

He chuckled. "That's bound to be a bestseller in Glory. The older houses in town have upward of a hundred fifty years of accumulated junk in their attics."

"All of which *someone* wants to buy. Thanks to the auction sites on the Internet, 'junk' is an obsolete concept. The trick is to locate the one person somewhere in the world who actually covets the trinket or doodad or knickknack your great-great grandmother stuffed into a cardboard box all those decades ago."

"Getting back to our problem…" Daniel began.

Sara interrupted. "I think you're being too hard on yourself. After all, fights about music in church are a recent phenomenon, a challenge that's caught pastors by surprise."

"Actually…" He spoke softly to avoid sounding like a schoolteacher giving a lecture. "Traditional music versus contemporary music has been a battleground for two thousand years. During the first century some Christians argued that the use of musical instruments of any kind during worship was either too much like the old Hebrew ceremonies or too pagan. Fifteen hundred years later the fight centered on whether secular music, harmony and folk melody should be banned from church, and whether all musical instruments except the organ should be eliminated."

Sara made a face. "I stand corrected. Our fight is clearly part of a long tradition, but I can't help feeling that the battle is unnecessary. We have two services, one traditional and one contemporary. The Caruthers bequest provides more than enough money to keep both sides happy."

"True. We have plenty of cash but only one sanctuary, which both groups want to redesign. That's really the crux of the disagreement."

She threw up her hands. "Exactly! The Traditionalists want it to look like a European cathedral. The Contemporaries want to give it the feel of a modern megachurch." She added, "The Traditionalists and the Contemporaries have both lost focus. We worship to please God, not ourselves."

"Both groups think they have that angle covered, too. Lily told me that God enjoys hymns and could not possibly be pleased with an insipid rock song that repeats the same simple words ten times over. Debbie Akers insists that God must be 'bored off his gourd,' as she put it, with a thousand years of dull hymn music and even duller words. Consequently, she says contemporary services have become wildly popular thanks to divine intervention."

Sara laughed. "I'm sorry, Daniel, but the battle at Glory Community does have a humorous side."

"I might have agreed with you a few months ago, but the truth is I don't find our fight funny anymore. I'm too worried that someone will get hurt."

Emma deftly carried a tray laden with an insulated carafe, two mugs and a plate of shortbread cookies as she led Simon Rogers to the gazebo in The Scottish Captain's back garden. The old wooden octagon was a pretty spot for a chat after breakfast, and also far enough away from the main house that it afforded a measure of privacy. The sun felt delightfully warm that Thursday morning. The weather forecast called for the temperature to climb into the high sixties by lunchtime.

"Thank you for rescuing me," Simon said. "The other travel writers in our group are going fishing for striped bass in Albemarle Sound. I would rather chew on ground glass. I would certainly get seasick and, with my bad luck, I would catch a dozen fish and be required to eat them."

"Assuming you could find someone to clean and cook them for you. We don't clean and fry fish for our guests at The Scottish Captain."

"Now I'm doubly glad I stayed behind. Today will be a perfect opportunity to recharge my batteries. There's a day trip to the Outer Banks tomorrow."

"Then you have no plans for this morning?"

"Not really. I shall pretend that I'm a road weary New England snowbird who decided to spend a down day in Glory, North Carolina. The tour of the grand houses and local museum yesterday was fascinating. I shall continue to browse around the town and soak up the ambience." He brushed a cookie crumb out of his beard. "With luck I'll find another Beetle on another porch."

Emma hoped that Simon didn't notice how she winced. The last thing Glory needed was a rowdy reputation among travel writers. Emma had her future tied up in The Scottish Captain. Her B and B must succeed and that would only happen if Glory prospered as she'd predicted it would.

"Please don't get the wrong idea about Glory," she said evenly. "We specialize in quiet, prank-free vacations."

"Oh yes, Glory is definitely a quiet place—which leads me to ask an impertinent question. Why would someone like you decide to abandon Seattle, a vibrant big city, and move to a pastoral southern town that even the Union Army avoided during the Civil War?"

The jolt of astonishment she felt came out as a nervous hiccup. She hadn't shared her biography with Simon Rogers, but he seemed to know a lot about her. Emma took a sip of coffee to help clear her throat. "You mentioned that I moved here from Seattle. Where did you come across that tidbit of information?"

"On the Internet, of course. Yesterday, I visited the Glory Public Library and typed your name into Google. Several 'hits' pointed to your biography." He grinned. "That's what happens when you become well-known enough in your field to make presentations at national hotel management conferences."

Emma bit her tongue. When she'd calmed down, she said, "My presenting days are over. I didn't realize that my bio was still online."

"Oh, yes, once on the Internet, information seems to linger forever. I must say that your hostelry credentials are impressive. As I recall, you earned your bachelor's degree from the prestigious Cornell University School of Hotel Administration, and you were appointed general manager of the Pacific Monarch Hotel in Seattle at the tender age of thirty-three. I've stayed at the Monarch—it's one of the most elegant hotels in the west. You obviously know your stuff."

Emma smiled. "Thank you. I like working in the hospitality business."

"I'm equally fascinated by your athletic prowess. Imagine, a champion women's softball pitcher serving us breakfast."

"I loved softball when I was a kid. I played on an intramural team at Cornell, and I joined a women's league in Seattle. My team, the Pacific Princesses, did manage to win the league championship three years ago. Softball is great fun and good exercise. End of story."

"To restate my original question in different words," Simon said, "why did you give up managing a world-class Seattle hotel and decide to run a small B and B?"

Emma tried to look thoughtful, as if she were pondering a difficult question. In fact, this was a question she had faced dozens of times, always with a pat answer that seemed to satisfy people—and had little to do with reality.

"After working in large hotels for more than a decade," she said, "I decided that I prefer the personal touch of managing a B and B. Back in Seattle, I dealt with crises from dawn to dusk. I had no time to think, much less talk to the guests. I prefer sharing a pot of coffee with you and enjoying a pleasant fall morning."

Simon grinned with apparent delight. Emma grinned back.

She could hear the conviction in her voice. She had become uncomfortably adept at avoiding the truth, but how could she admit that her chief motivation for moving to North Carolina's coastal Albemarle Region was its distance from Seattle, Washington? A small B and B in a dot-on-the-map town seemed the last place in the country that her ex-husband or his vast family would ever visit.

More to the point, Emma thought, the "truth" was rapidly becoming irrelevant. So what if she ran away from a bad situation? After a year at The Scottish Captain her perspective changed. She now realized that she'd actually run *toward* a much happier life.

Emma poured a second mug of coffee for Simon.

"Now, as for choosing Glory," she went on, "I applied every scrap of economic forecasting and financial-planning experience I'd acquired working at large hotels. I concluded that Glory is an undiscovered treasure, an unspoiled little town with lots to see and do, that is destined to become a highly regarded attraction. I invested every cent of my savings in The Scottish Captain. I truly believe that I selected the right place at the right time."

Emma punctuated her words with an emphatic nod. Here, she was expressing the way she really felt, even though she knew that little Glory was still overshadowed by its well-known neighbors. Edenton, some twenty miles west, had more history to offer tourists—including its own Revolutionary-era "tea party." And Elizabeth City, fifteen miles north, was the region's commercial center, a popular stopping point for yachtsmen traversing the Dismal Swamp Canal on the Intracoastal Waterway.

"I agree with you," Simon said. "Glory is a surprising little town, and I am difficult to surprise. What has impressed me most are the people I've met so far. Really top notch. Lots of fascinating characters."

"Characters?"

"That came out badly. Let me start again." He poured cream into his mug and stirred. "Travel writing is fun, but I don't want to mass-produce travel articles for the rest of my life. I hope to write fiction some day. Consequently, I've made it a habit to make note of interesting people who have the potential to become great characters in a novel. Glory added several new possibilities to my collection."

"So that's how novelists do it," she said. "You adapt real-life people."

"Sure. A good example is Glory's high school football coach. I met him yesterday morning. He's a hoot."

"Tom Yeager," she said with a sigh. "A man who knows how to strike a tough bargain."

"Exactly! He's an unusual blend of zeal, skill, confidence and cunning. That's what makes him a good coach."

Emma saw no point in arguing with Simon, who clearly thought himself a great judge of character. He wouldn't want to hear that the Glory Gremlins had a losing record that most townsfolk blamed on Tom Yeager's lack of coaching skill. "Who else have you met?"

"Sam Lange, the fellow who owns the Glory Book Nook. I don't think I've come across a more knowledgeable book expert anywhere, and I love to visit bookstores. The fascinating thing about Sam is that he combines great expertise with a healthy dose of curmudgeonly behavior." Simon threw back his head and laughed. "And I wouldn't have it any other way. A sour temper is an integral part of his persona. It's like the splash of malt vinegar on a plate of fish and chips."

"Very perceptive." Emma drank from her mug and imagined the "recipe" that Simon might assign to her. Mix a can of hospitality with a cup of wishful thinking. Season with a dash of rotten luck in choosing a husband, then bake for thirty-seven years. Yields one healthy serving of Emma McCall. Or perhaps he didn't see her as a fascinating character. "Did anyone else in town catch your literary eye?"

"Rafe Neilson, of course. A cop in a small town, but hardly a small-town cop. I could write a whole novel about the past five years of his life."

"Really? I don't know much about him," she said, then immediately regretted her choice of words. They made her sound disconnected from the rest of Glory.

Simon hadn't noticed her gaffe. He was far too busy retelling what he had learned about Rafe the day before. Emma settled back in her chair and let him prattle away.

The things I have to put up with to run a bed-and-breakfast.

FIVE

The black-and-white felt clunky compared to the Corvette, but it had the definite advantage of looking like a police car on patrol. Rafe turned right onto Princes Street and drove north at the leisurely pace of fifteen miles per hour. There wasn't much chance of catching a culprit in the act, but the presence of three police cruisers circulating through downtown Glory—his car, Angie Ringgold's car and a police department SUV driven by Rafe's subordinate Sergeant Myers—should dampen the enthusiasm of any high school students planning new pranks.

"Our plan seems to be working so far," he murmured as he approached Main Street. "Not a single incident yet this morning." He nosed into the intersection, looked to the right and caught a glimpse of Angie making the sharp left turn to Water Street. Since she was heading toward the northeast quadrant of town, he decided to patrol the streets to the south. He turned west on Main Street and then south on Broad Street. Ahead on his left was The Scottish Captain.

Rafe let the cruiser slow to a crawl. He had some

good news for Emma and planned to telephone her later that morning.

Since I'm outside her B and B, maybe I should I pay her a visit instead.

Rafe noted that Emma's Volvo wagon occupied its usual spot in the parking lot. That probably meant that she was working inside the building.

Where else would she be at half-past nine in the morning?

The morning was a busy time at a B and B. Emma might be cleaning up after breakfast. She probably had countless other small chores to do. A phone call might be more convenient for her.

Convenient, but also impersonal.

Rafe thought about Emma's circumstances. She had lived in Glory for the better part of a year but remained oddly disengaged from the rest of the town. She hadn't bothered to make many friends, and she didn't seem to have a boyfriend. She even chose not to become a member of Glory Community Church.

Why not pay her a visit? It won't take much time. In fact, you ought to think about inviting her to a friendly dinner before next week's choir practice.

He steered to the curb, killed the ignition and thought about the appropriate "Ten code" to use in this situation. He keyed the small microphone pinned to his lapel. "Dispatcher, Car Oh-One going ten-ten for about fifteen minutes. My ten-twenty is 18 Broad Street."

A female voice replied, "Acknowledged. Car Oh-One out of service, with radio on. Your location is 18 Broad Street. Please notify when you go ten-eight again."

Rafe clipped his handheld radio to his belt and climbed out of the cruiser. He followed the flagstone path to the rear of The Scottish Captain and peered through the window in the back door. Emma sat at a desk in the kitchen working on some kind of list. Like yesterday, she wore a T-shirt and a pair of blue jeans.

She really does look lovely when she's dressed in simple clothing.

He stepped back and tapped on the door.

"Who is it?" she bellowed, clearly not in a mood to be disturbed.

"Rafe Neilson," he said. "I come bearing happy news."

He heard a heartfelt groan, then heavy footsteps. She flung open the door. "You have an amazing knack for visiting at the worst possible times. I'm leaving for Elizabeth City at one for a meeting with a new food supplier. I have less than an hour to inventory my pantry and figure out the food items I need for December, the most complicated food month there is, because of Christmas."

Rafe doubted that a hectic morning was responsible for the near anger he could hear in her voice. Emma sounded mad at him.

"I'll be brief," he said evenly. "Expect to receive a call later this afternoon from Tom Yeager. I explained to him that the Glory Gremlins were responsible for moving the Beetle to your porch. He has decided, as he put it, to 'reopen the negotiations' on the number of weekends you'll donate to the team's fund-raising campaign."

Instead of smiling, Emma merely nodded. Rafe felt cheated by her response. Instead of saying thank-you, she made a grunt.

Why doesn't she act more pleased by my news?

He continued talking, "If you wanted to, I suppose, you could withdraw the entire offer—but I suggest you whittle it down to one weekend."

Another grunt.

"In that case, let me ask what's bothering you. You're evidently annoyed at me, but I have no idea why. Can you fill me in?"

"Since you asked..." Emma shook her head sadly. "Last night, you let me believe you're a small-town cop. Why didn't you tell me that you used to be a big-city cop, that you moved to Glory after your wife was killed during the 9/11 attack on the World Trade Center?" She uttered a quiet sigh. "I had to hear about your previous life—and your terrible loss—from a travel reporter who's in Glory on a three-day trip."

Rafe inhaled sharply. He hadn't expected Emma's question and felt blindsided by it.

"The subject never came up during our conversation," he said softly. "My past isn't a secret. All my friends know that I moved here from Long Island. Most folks at church know." He took another breath. "Besides, I wasn't a big-city cop. I worked for the New York State Police. I was a plainclothes detective in the Bureau of Criminal Investigation."

Rafe lifted his hand in a "that's the whole story" gesture. He prayed that Emma would not probe further into his past. Talking about his wife dredged up too many painful memories. Kim had been working on the ninety-second floor of the North Tower—the target that the first 767-200 hit at 8:45 a.m.

"I seem to be the only person in town who didn't know about you," she said. "I must have come across as both stupid and insensitive when we spoke."

"That's not true. You did neither."

"Look, I'm sorry, Rafe. Your life history is really none of my business. I have to get back to work."

Rafe watched the back door swing shut in his face. *That went well. Now I feel like a total dunce.*

He had almost reached the end of the flagstone path when his radio squawked. "Rafe, it's Angie. There's been another prank. A real doozy."

"Where?"

"Drive west on Campbell Street. Look for people standing outside on the sidewalk. Including Chief Porter and me."

Rafe took a moment to contemplate the stupidity of this particular prankster. He—or she—had executed a practical joke at the Glory Police Headquarters.

Emma climbed out of her Volvo at 4:30 p.m. feeling tired but productive. The new food supplier in Elizabeth City had surprised her with the depth and breadth of his inventory. He carried many gourmet foods imported from Europe and Asia. She had written a check for more than a thousand dollars and now looked forward to weekly deliveries of rare ingredients that would enable her to serve even more elegant breakfasts.

"The B and B professor would be proud of me," Emma murmured, as she walked toward the Captain's back door. She often thought about the corpulent instructor who led the "How to Run a Successful Bed-and-Breakfast" seminar she'd attended in Boston the year before. She had forgotten the man's name, but not his enthusiasm.

"Repeat after me," he had insisted. "Bed-and-breakfast." He waited until the roomful of future innkeepers had responded. "Say it again with gusto. *Bed-and-breakfast!*"

He had slapped his podium with his chubby right palm in rhythm with the four syllables. "The bed-and-breakfast is a fabulous concept in hospitality created by marrying two basic necessities. A bed. And a breakfast."

The rotund expert had paused for effect before he went on. "Which of the two will be the more significant driver of your success as an innkeeper? Many of you might be tempted to say the bed. My friends, you would be wrong. A good night's sleep is certainly important, but the typical guest quickly forgets about the bed you provide unless it is lumpy, soggy, bug-ridden, or otherwise not fit to sleep in. On the other hand—" he had made a sweeping gesture with his well-manicured left hand "—your guests will long remember and tell their friends repeatedly about a glorious breakfast. *Never* forget that simple truth."

The kitchen door suddenly swung open in front of her.

"I've been waiting for you to get back, Mizz McCall," Hancock Jeffers said. He added the slight bow he offered at the start of all of their conversations.

"Is anything wrong, Hancock?" Emma had "inherited" Hancock Jeffers when she purchased The Scottish Captain. Carole and Duncan Frasier had made it a requirement of the deal that she keep Hancock on as the Captain's handyman, gardener and jack-of-all-trades. He was hardworking and scrupulously punctual, arriving at eight each morning and going home at four every afternoon.

"Frankly," Carole had said to Emma, "you'd be lost without him. Hancock has tended this building for more than fifty years. He knows the place better than anyone else in Glory."

Duncan took over. "We've never been able to find out how old he is. His employment paperwork gives his age as seventy-one, but he's probably over eighty."

Duncan smiled. "You'll find that Hancock doesn't say much, but whenever he talks, it pays to listen carefully."

Emma checked her watch again. What had made Hancock hang around an extra half hour?

"Well…nothing's definitely *wrong,* ma'am. But everything sure ain't right."

Emma struggled not to smile. Hancock Jeffers put phrases together much like the great Yogi Berra did. He occasionally said things that sounded illogical on the surface, but made good sense in a wacky sort of way.

"I see." Emma nodded. "Something strange happened this afternoon that *might* be a problem."

"Something uncommonly strange, ma'am."

"Let's have some coffee while we talk about it."

"Yes, ma'am," he said, with unmistakable glee. "French vanilla, if you please."

This time, she let herself smile. Hancock enjoyed the flavored coffees produced by the new pod coffeemaker Emma had bought. The one-cup-at-a-time pods were less expensive than keeping a large coffee urn filled all day for guests and staff. They also offered more variety.

She led him to the mini kitchen area in the corner of the rear first-floor parlor, the smaller of the two parlors. It was available all day for guests who wanted coffee or a snack. He sat down at the small, round, glass-topped dining table.

Emma looked at Hancock's distorted image in the coffeemaker's shiny chrome exterior. He was compact, wiry and strong, with a leathery complexion that came from working many years in the strong North Carolina sun. His big ears looked even larger because he was completely bald. He favored old South formality, wore long-sleeved shirts on the hottest days and insisted on calling Emma "Miz McCall" or ma'am. He expected his employer to address him as Hancock in return—never Mr. Jeffers.

Emma slid a mug of French vanilla coffee across the table to Hancock. "Tell me about the strange happening," she said.

"Well, ma'am," he said, after taking a long sip, "about an hour after you left, Miz Lily Kirk knocked on the front door. She said she had an appointment to see you."

"What appointment?" Emma heard the astonishment in her voice and added, "I mean that I don't recall making an appointment with Lily. In fact, she knew that I would be gone this afternoon—I told her so last night."

"I told her you'd gone to Elizabeth City, and I explained that you keep a calendar in a little computer gizmo you carry in your purse. I also said that I've never known you to forget an appointment with anyone."

"And I never will," Emma said firmly. "What happened then?"

He sighed. "She said, 'Hancock, maybe I did make a mistake, but I still need to see Emma McCall. I'll wait in the parlor until she gets back.' She walked past me and went into the front parlor. No way I could stop her."

Emma pictured the hefty Lily bulldozing past Hancock. "I suppose not. When Lily has made her mind up, the only thing to do is to step out of the way."

Hancock gave a slight shrug. "I figured that Mizz Kirk's beginning to go soft in the head. Happens to some folks when they get old. Well, I made sure she was comfortable in the parlor. I made her a cup of tea, and I brought her a stack of new magazines."

"Very thoughtful."

Hancock grinned. "Thank you, ma'am." The grin faded. "Then an hour later I went back to check on her. She was gone. She left without a word."

"I suppose she decided not to wait for me. She told me she'd be here this evening. Maybe she decided to talk later."

"Maybe…" Hancock sounded hesitant to continue. He paused for a moment then went on. "I didn't see her leave, and I was working in the front yard. Mizz Kirk must have used the back door and then squeezed past the hedge in the rear garden. I would have seen her depart by any other route."

"Squeezed past a hedge? That is odd."

He nodded slowly. "Odd enough that I began to wonder if Mizz Kirk might have…ah, *borrowed* something from the Captain. That might explain why she left the way she did."

Emma thought about it. Could Hancock be right? Lily Kirk didn't appear to be a thief—but that didn't mean much. She had definitely acted strangely the evening before. In fact, she had perked up at the news that Emma would be gone….

Don't be silly. Lily Kirk isn't a thief. There has to be another explanation for her weird behavior.

"Hancock, we have several antiques worth *borrowing* in our front parlor, but since Lily didn't have a moving van with her today I doubt that she took anything."

"Yes, ma'am." He smiled sheepishly. "I must admit that when I looked around the room, I didn't find anything missing."

Emma stood up. "Thank you for telling me about Lily. The best way to sort out the mystery is to talk to

Lily and ask the purpose of her visit. I'll pull her aside this evening..."

The *thud* of the front door slamming silenced Emma in midsentence. She spun around in time to catch a glimpse of Simon Rogers striding down the hallway, a sour expression on his face.

"Mr. Rogers?" she called.

No response.

Emma moved quickly into the hallway and tried again. "Simon!" He climbed halfway up the stairs to the second floor before he turned around.

"This town is a grotesque hazard to life and limb." He seemed to spit his words at Emma. "The faster I leave, the longer I'll stay healthy."

"What hap—" she began to say. Simon cut her off.

"You ask what happened." He paused to amplify the drama in his oration. "What happened is that your stupid Phantom Avenger almost killed me. I was visiting Police Headquarters when the latest prank went down. An old-fashioned stink bomb exploded and filled the building with a sulfur compound that smelled like rotten eggs."

"Oh, dear."

"I'll say! The trouble is that I'm unusually allergic to sulfur compounds. I started wheezing and hacking, developed an instant headache and nearly passed out. They had to cart me to your rinky-dink hospital in a police car. Once there, of course, your crew of small-town, so-called doctors didn't know what to do to make me comfortable. I told them I needed a shot of epinephrine, but they kept dragging their feet. No thanks to them, I recovered and fled that den of medical incompetence. Once I get back to civilization, I intend to get checked out by a real physician at a real hospital. Naturally, I'll send the bill to the Glory Tourist and Convention Bureau."

Emma tried to think quickly. "There's really no need to shorten your visit to Glory, Simon. These pranks are an aberration. Won't you give Glory a chance to restore itself to your good graces? At least enjoy a pleasant dinner. Then decide whether or not to leave."

"Oh, I intend to have a pleasant dinner—in Greenville. In fact, I'll be meeting with a TV reporter, an old friend of mine, who wants me to tell him everything I know about the Phantom Avenger."

Emma watched Simon clomp upstairs while his angry words echoed in her mind. She began to imagine the horrific tale he would spin for his old friend—how he cheated a malodorous death by the slenderest of circumstances. Then she pictured the TV news feature that might appear tomorrow evening—a grim account of vandalism perpetrated by teenage gangs running wild in Glory, North Carolina, a bad situation made worse by the town's shoddy medical services. A story like that combined with the "hard-hitting article" that Rex Grainger planned to run in tomorrow's *Glory Gazette* could be enough to frighten away flocks of Northern snowbirds…and lots of future vacationers.

"This is intolerable!" Emma shouted at the now-empty staircase. "The Phantom Avenger will drive the Captain out of business." She turned when she heard Hancock Jeffers gasp behind her.

"Is the Captain in trouble, Miz McCall?" His usually cheerful face now burned with concern. "I wouldn't want to see that."

"Forgive me, Hancock." She forced herself to smile.

"I'm upset and angry and said the first thing that popped into my mind. Trust me, the Captain is in fine condition."

"I wish I could say the same for Glory," she muttered quietly.

Emma kept smiling as Hancock left for home. She even managed to maintain the plastered-on grin as Simon Rogers, suitcase in hand, clomped back down the staircase, flung open the front door and made for his car—without uttering a goodbye or a thank-you.

She made a snap decision. *It's about time I complained to the police. The Phantom Avenger deserves to be in jail.*

Emma locked the front door behind her as she left. She walked north on Broad Street in the fading sunlight and thought about the brilliant arguments she would make to Rafe Neilson—*scratch that!*—the brilliant arguments she would make to *Chief Porter.*

One—it's absolutely essential that the police keep Glory the kind of town that tourists will want to visit. Anything less, and tourism—Glory's single most important industry—will crash and burn.

Two—while the Phantom Avenger's pranks are less serious than the crimes one sees in many big cities, spraying our Police Headquarters with smelly chemicals is intolerable—even if Simon Rogers is an overblown hypochondriac.

Three—Rafe Neilson probably exceeded the limits of his discretion when he chose not to arrest the perpetrators of the more dangerous practical jokes. If he's not sure whether a prank is a crime, he should check with the local county attorney.

Emma, busy fighting mental skirmishes, didn't notice that she had turned left on Campbell Street until she began to smell a foul odor in the air. She paused to get her bearings. The Glory Police Headquarters was fifty yards ahead. A large, white-panel truck was parked in front of the old one-story redbrick building. The sign on the truck's side read MacIntyre Industrial Cleaners.

Emma noted that the rank smell grew more pungent as she neared the police building. The front door and windows were open, the shades fully raised. She could make out several people in white coveralls, masks covering their faces, working in different rooms—but no policemen.

Where are the cops?

Emma approached the front door and peered cautiously around the jamb. The stench was considerably stronger here. She wondered if she should step inside.

A familiar voice behind her said, "If I were you, I wouldn't go any farther. The Phantom Avenger stinkbombed the building."

Emma turned. Rafe seemed angrier than he'd been when he had shown up unannounced at the Captain.

Good. Now maybe the police will take action.

"Did the Avenger leave a note?" she asked.

He nodded. "A not-very-creative one. It read, 'Some of us think that traditional music stinks. The Phantom Avenger strikes again.'" He made a face. "The device itself was quite clever. He or she cobbled together a timer, a battery, an electric valve and a bottle full of a really smelly chemical, then placed the device on the steel bulkhead door on the side of our building. At nine-thirty this morning, the valve opened and the liquid dribbled into the basement. A few minutes later, vapors rose to the first floor and settled on everything in sight. We had to bring in a cleaning crew to scrub down our walls and floor." He added, "This is not a good time to pay us a visit."

"Perhaps not," Emma said, "but I need to speak with Chief Porter. The sooner the better."

Rafe frowned. "He went to the scene of a motor vehicle accident. Try again tomorrow."

"No— I want to lodge a complaint today. I suppose I can talk to you, instead."

Rafe shook his head. "Sorry, but I'm on my way to the same accident."

She tried to read Rafe's grim expression. Was this a brush-off?

"What's so important about a fender bender that all our police brass are rushing off to see it?"

Rafe took a moment to answer. "More than a fender got bent. Lily Kirk drove her Ford Taurus into a ditch on State Route 34A. She's dead."

SIX

Rafe decided to drive Code 3 to the scene of Lily Kirk's accident—lights blazing, siren blaring—mostly to take his mind off Emma McCall. The woman was exasperating… No! *Infuriating,* was a better word. Now she intended to annoy the Chief.

Stop thinking about her. You have police work to do.

Rafe accelerated when Main Street became State Route 34A at the Glory town limit. Lily had died four miles northwest of Glory on an especially perilous section of highway that passed through a dense stand of pine trees. Rafe's daughter had nicknamed that stretch "the forest primeval," but he knew that the real danger to motorists came not from tree trunks but from the deep ditches on either side of the road. He slowed his cruiser when he spotted blinking red-and-blue lights ahead.

Rafe made a U-turn and steered onto the narrow shoulder. He whistled softly when he saw the accident scene that was illuminated by two portable floodlights. Lily's old Taurus had landed nose first in the ditch, lifting its rear wheels five feet off the ground. The car's hood and trunk were both open. The little that Rafe could see of the car's front end reminded him of a crumpled soda can.

Two North Carolina State Highway Patrol cars were strategically parked to discourage rubbernecking by blocking the view of the wreck to southbound drivers. Chief Porter and one of the troopers were waving traffic past the scene. A second trooper was renewing a line of highway flares along the edge of the southbound lane. Rafe recognized her at once despite the garish red light—Corporal Sandy Lennox, a tall woman who always looked right at home under her trooper hat and reflective sunglasses. This evening, though, Rafe had a clear view of her eyes as he approached her. He was astonished to see tears glistening on her cheeks.

"Hi, Rafe." She uncapped a flare and scratched its igniter button. The flare began to spit red sparks. She positioned the flare on a wire stand and took a moment to blow her nose. Then she smiled at Rafe.

"You're probably wondering," she said, "why a case-hardened Highway Patrol trooper is sniffing at the scene of a traffic accident."

Rafe returned Sandy's smile. "I admit some curiosity."

"I liked Lily Kirk. When I worked the night shift, she was one of my regular customers. I personally gave her two citations for speeding and three more for not wearing her seat belt. I warned her that she'd kill herself if she didn't mend her ways." Sandy heaved a sigh. "Be glad you got here *after* the Medical Examiner left with the body. Lily hit the steering column hard enough to collapse it—and shatter every bone in her torso."

"Any thoughts on the sequence of events?" Rafe asked cautiously. Sandy sounded as though she wanted to keep talking about the accident.

The trooper nodded. "There's no mystery at all. Lily was barreling toward Glory at seventy, maybe seventy-five, when her hood popped up and blocked her forward vision. She hit the brakes hard about there." Sandy pointed toward a spot a hundred yards up the road. "You can see the streak of rubber her tires left on the pavement. Then she skidded into the ditch. That's when the trunk lid opened up, too."

"Seems simple enough."

"We have a witness who saw the whole thing—the driver of a FedEx delivery truck who called in the accident. Lily passed him—in a no passing zone, of course—and was picking up speed when he heard a loud noise and the hood sprang open. He said the Taurus seemed to fly into the ditch."

"A loud noise? From what?"

The trooper blinked away another tear. "Probably the sound of the latch giving way. My guess is that the hood *bounced* open when she hit a bump in the road. Check the latch. It's bent and rusty. Lily wasn't big on periodic maintenance, either."

Rafe looked at the sky. The sun would be setting in less than a half hour, but there was still enough light to survey the wreck. He skidded down the side of the five-foot-deep ditch. The ground near Lily's car was strewn with books, some with their spines broken, pages fluttering in the breeze. He spotted more books inside the open trunk.

He stepped over the scattered tomes, taking in details as he circumnavigated the totaled Taurus. The car's four tires were still inflated—Lily hadn't experienced a blowout. The side windows were intact, indicating that the car hadn't rolled over. The driver's door had been pried open, undoubtedly by the Medical Examiner's people to remove Lily's body. The steering wheel now rested against the bottom of the dashboard. The driver's side windshield, dappled with specks of red, had shattered where Lily's head had struck the glass. And the front hood latch, he observed, was indeed bent and rusty.

What more did you expect to see? he wondered, as he began to climb out of the ditch. *The Highway Patrol knows lots more about single-car accidents than you do.*

"Let me give you a hand," Sandy said. Rafe stretched out his arm; her pulling strength impressed him. He scrambled up the ditch's grassy wall in three easy steps.

"You guys do good work…" Rafe began, when he heard the sound of tires rolling on gravel. He turned in time to see Emma's Volvo wagon slow to a stop twenty feet away. The driver's side window was rolled down.

"This is an accident scene, Miss McCall," he shouted. "Please move on."

Emma didn't speak, merely shook her head as she climbed out of the Volvo. Her cheeks looked pale, Rafe thought, as if she was getting ready to faint.

Great! We'll need an ambulance for an unwanted gawker.

"You'll slow down our work if you stay here, Emma." He didn't try to keep the annoyance out of his voice. "Please get back into your car. I'd rather not have to arrest you."

Emma stood her ground. "I'm here to talk to the Chief. This is a crime scene, not an accident scene."

Rafe swallowed a groan. He moved toward her and said, "As you can see, the Chief is busy. If you plan to waste his time with nonsense, talk to me."

Rafe saw Emma's face darken. "I'll be happy to,

Officer. I met with Lily last night after choir practice. She told me that someone driving a pickup truck tried to run her off the road yesterday. She was frightened."

"But not enough to report the incident to the police."

"True, because she thought you'd laugh at her, that you'd see her story as the product of hysteria and paranoia." Emma crossed her arms on her chest. "Now, may I finish my story?"

Rafe thought about objecting but merely grunted. He glanced around. Sandy Lennox had retreated to her vehicle and was talking on her radio.

Why did I offer to listen to this nonsense?

Emma went on. "Lily showed up unannounced at The Scottish Captain this afternoon. I assume that she wanted to tell me more about her fears. Unfortunately, I wasn't there." She gestured toward the wreck. "Her death a few hours later is too much of a coincidence."

Rafe stared into Emma's blue eyes and forced himself to speak calmly. "I don't know what—if anything—occurred yesterday. Given Lily's driving habits, it's more likely that she would run another driver off the road. But this was a genuine accident. We have a witness who saw Lily go into the ditch."

Emma frowned. "What kind of witness?"

"A FedEx driver. He saw the hood of the Taurus come open. That's why Lily lost control. Had she been wearing a seat belt she might have survived the crash."

"Oh." The mention of a witness seemed to soften Emma's belligerent tone. She began to inspect the mangled Taurus then suddenly seemed to notice the books lying nearby in the ditch. "Did those books come from Lily's car?"

Rafe nodded. "Yep. They were undoubtedly on their way to the Glory Book Nook."

Emma seemed puzzled. "I don't understand."

"It's another zinger in John Caruthers's will. He left fifty boxes of old books to Sam Lange, subject to a condition. The church can choose any ten books of interest for its library. Because Lily Kirk was a retired librarian, she ended up with the task of picking the church's ten books. As I understand it, she carted another trunkload of books to Sam every few days. What you see here must be the current batch."

"Old books are fascinating," she started to say. She began again, "Oh, my! I forgot about tonight."

"Tonight?"

"Sara Knoll's writers' club is supposed to meet at the Captain. The topic is Sara's current book. Lily planned to attend. Half the members of the club also belong to Glory Community Church." Emma peered at Rafe. "Did you announce Lily's death?"

"Not yet. We're trying to locate her next of kin, although I don't think Lily had any surviving relatives."

"I didn't know she was all alone." A look of sadness crossed Emma's face and abruptly changed to an expression of resolve. "Can I tell Sara Knoll about the...*accident?* I'm sure she'll want to cancel the meeting."

Another round of tire noise on gravel caught Rafe's attention. He looked behind Emma as a flatbed tow truck rolled to a stop alongside the ditch.

"Feel free to tell the world," Rafe said to Emma. "Everyone will figure out that Lily's gone when Tucker Mackenzie drives through Glory with the remains of her Taurus strapped to his truck."

Rafe tugged Emma several steps backward to give Tucker room to maneuver his big rig. She whirled around to look at the long, green vehicle, and then asked, "Where will you take Lily's car?"

"To the impound lot at the Glory Garage. We'll have it checked out for mechanical failures that might have contributed to the accident."

Emma seemed satisfied by the explanation, although Rafe noted a curious glint of determination in her eyes. "I'd better go back to the Captain," she said, "and make that phone call."

Rafe watched Emma return to the Volvo and wondered what she *really* intended to do. She seemed too attached to the crazy notion that Lily had been run off the road to give up so easily.

"You have other plans," he murmured. "I can feel it."

Emma stopped a mile down State Route 34A to jot down the two pieces of information she wanted to remember. *Tucker Mackenzie* and *Glory Garage.* Then she waited, engine idling, on the sandy shoulder of the road for the tow truck to go by. She used her cell phone to call Sara Knoll, who said she would notify the members of the writers' club about Lily's death and tell them that the meeting was canceled.

Twenty-five minutes later, the big flatbed truck rumbled past her vantage point. She put the Volvo in gear and followed the truck into Glory.

Emma had often driven past Glory Garage's driveway on King Street, but she'd never realized that the garage and its various parking lots occupied much of the interior of the block defined by Queen Street on the west, King Street on the east, MacTavish Lane on the north and

Oliver Street on the south. She parked next to a squat brick building that housed the office and the four-bay garage. It was past six and dark, but several floodlights on stanchions illuminated the interior pavement.

Tucker Mackenzie began waving as he descended from the truck cab. "I'm sorry, ma'am, the garage closed at five."

"It's me, Tucker," she said. "Emma McCall. I followed you back from the accident scene."

He gazed at her for a few seconds. "Oh, yeah. You were with Deputy Chief Neilson." Tucker quickly drew his right palm across his pant leg then offered his hand. Emma bit back a smile. Somewhere in Tucker's past, the women in his life must have complained about grease.

"You own one of the B and Bs in town, don't you?" he asked.

"The Scottish Captain."

"That's right—the Captain." He gave a little nod. "I'm pleased to meet you, though I wish it was under happier circumstances." He glanced over his shoulder at the crushed car on the truck. "What a terrible shame. Poor Lily. She might have survived if she'd worn her seat belt."

"Actually, that's why I'm here. I'd like to examine Lily's car."

"Uh…" Tucker seemed at a loss for words. "*Examine* the Taurus? In what way?"

Emma tried her best to generate a friendly smile. "Let me begin again. I'd like to examine the car with your help." She looked directly at Tucker. She intended to be truthful with him, and she wanted the man to look her in the eyes. "Last night, Lily told me that a big pickup truck came up behind her and tried to push the Taurus off State Route 34A."

"Oh, wow!" Tucker seemed to gasp. "Do you think she could have been exaggerating?"

"Lily said the truck made a dent in the back bumper."

Tucker, a tall, stocky man in his late fifties, raced to the back of his tow truck at a speed that amazed Emma. He retrieved a flashlight from his pocket and began to inspect the bumper.

"I suppose that big dent on the left side could be fresh, but it's hard to tell with a car this old." He switched off the flashlight. "It doesn't matter anyway. The troopers told me that this was a single-car accident. Lily drove into a ditch today without any help from a pickup truck."

"I'm worried about other possibilities." Emma looked Tucker squarely in the eye. "Would you be able to tell if Lily's car had been tampered with?"

Tucker frowned. "You mean…intentional *sabotage?* Maybe like fiddling with her brakes?"

"I was thinking more of a prank, or a practical joke."

"Ah…" Tucker's frown deepened as he grasped Emma's meaning. "You're wondering if the Phantom Avenger did something nasty to the car."

She nodded. "Lily was a leader on the opposite side of the dispute. It's quite possible that she would be the target of a prank." Emma hoped her incomplete explanation would suffice; she wasn't in the mood to explain the fight between the Contemporaries and Traditionalists. She barely understood the conflict herself.

"Well…there's only one way to find out." Tucker moved to a bank of control levers on the side of the tow truck. Emma watched as two hydraulic cylinders lifted the front of the flatbed and brought the rear edge close to the ground. She edged back from the truck as an electric winch unwound and allowed the wrecked Taurus to roll onto the pavement.

Emma needed a moment to appreciate that the car looked dramatically different because its hood was no longer attached to the body.

"Where's the hood?" she asked.

"I had to remove it." Tucker pointed to a battered sheet-metal object tied to the front of the flatbed. "The crash sprung the hinges and support arms, so the silly thing wouldn't come down." Tucker switched his flashlight on again and illuminated the front of the Taurus. "Of course, even if it had closed, the hood latch was on its last legs. It probably gave way when she hit a bump. That's what the police think caused the accident. The Chief asked me to check the latch out."

Emma leaned forward for a closer look. "I presume the hooklike gizmo holds the hood down and shut."

"Yep." He shifted the beam a few inches to the right. "There's supposed to be a secondary safety latch about there, but it's gone. Probably snapped off because Lily slammed the hood once too often." He gave his head an unhappy shake. "Sometimes women just don't understand how to care for the cars they drive."

Emma could see no advantage to arguing with Tucker's clear-cut chauvinism, or to reminding him how much Lily loved her Taurus. She decided to change the subject. "Can we browse around inside the engine compartment?"

"Sure thing." Tucker began to move the flashlight beam slowly around the engine compartment. Emma tried to catalog in her mind what she saw. The high-performance engine looked reasonably clean, but many nearby components were coated with grime, and more than a few with rust. Emma glanced at Tucker. He didn't seem unduly surprised by the sights that had been hidden beneath the old car's hood.

He made eye contact with her. "Do you have any idea what kind of damage we're looking for?"

"Not really. What might a prankster do to a car that could cause the hood to open without warning?"

"Well, I suppose you could file down the latch, or misadjust the release lever."

"You sound doubtful."

"Look at the latch—no file marks." He moved the rusty part back and forth on its pivot. "There's plenty of motion, so no one fooled with the release lever."

Emma peered at the engine, wondering if she was wasting both their time. Perhaps the police were right. Maybe Lily hit a bump in the road. Except…

"I admit I don't know much about cars," she said, "but is it that easy to bounce open an unlatched hood?"

"Sure. She'd have to hit a big bump head-on—or drive over a small bump at unusually high speed."

"I drive State Route 34A two or three times a week. That stretch of road is smooth as custard."

Tucker shrugged. "Well, if the springs in the support arms were worn, even a gentle bounce might be enough to pop the hood. I'll check them, also." He turned his attention back to illuminating the engine compartment.

This time, Emma noticed a sprinkling of red spots atop the grime as the flashlight beam moved across and around the engine of the Taurus. She stepped closer to the wreck.

"What do you suppose those bits of red are?" she said.

"Bits of red?" Tucker echoed. "Where are you looking?"

"There." She took his arm and guided the flashlight beam. "On the left side of the engine, near the bottom."

He leaned over the ruined fender. "Yeah, I can see your red bits..." He paused and began again. "I'd say they're little scraps of paper. What's more, I think they're charred around the edges." His voice became louder. "Hey! I found something else down here—just below the engine, hanging from a thin wire."

"What?"

"Beats me." He added, "I'll try to pull it free."

Emma heard the twang of a metal wire breaking. Tucker stood up. He held the flashlight in his right hand and a splintered cardboard tube—the size of a frankfurter—in his left. At first, Emma thought the tube had been painted red. But then she realized that it was wrapped with a layer of thin red paper. The tube's mangled edges were charred black, and two thin insulated wires protruded from one end.

"If I had to guess," she said, "I'd say you found the remains of giant firecracker. That's what the little ones look like after they go off."

Tucker began to smile. "You're *almost* right, ma'am. I haven't seen one of these babies for a good forty years. We called 'em 'big-bang noisemakers' when I was a kid. They explode when the—*ah,* victim starts his car. It really is a funny prank. In fact, I still remember the expression on old Mr. McConnell's face when he turned the key..."

Emma interrupted him. "How big is the 'big bang'? Is it strong enough to lift a car's hood?"

She watched Tucker's eyes widen in recognition. "You bet it is! I've seen it happen. These noisemakers pack a huge wallop. More than enough to lift a hood that's not properly latched down." Almost immediately, his expression changed. He peered quizzically at the red cardboard contraption. "But it *didn't* explode when Lily turned the key. I wonder why not."

"I'm sure the police will figure that out," she said. "We have a more pressing question to answer. Where's the note from the Phantom Avenger?"

Emma almost yanked the flashlight out of Tucker's hand. There had to be a note. Every stupid prank of late had been accompanied by a smug letter signed by the Phantom Avenger.

She scanned the engine compartment. Perhaps the note was taped to the inner fender…or inside an envelope tucked behind the battery…or folded small and squeezed into the engine's air filter.

Nothing.

"That's impossible," she said, to no one. "There's always a note. Where are you hiding?"

Tucker stepped around Emma and said, "I'll find a plastic evidence bag for the noisemaker." He sounded uncertain how else to respond to her rhetorical question. She watched him walk away into the dark, then decided to use the opportunity to examine the car's misshapen interior.

Emma flinched as the flashlight illuminated dried blood on the black leather seat. She swung the beam back into the engine compartment and murmured, "Where else could the Phantom Avenger have put the note?"

Her gaze traveled to the upended hood on the still-tilted flatbed. There it was—a large white file card secured by two lengths of duct tape. How had Tucker managed to miss it when he pried the hood loose from the car?

Emma moved next to the flatbed, craned her neck and managed to read the neatly printed words: "We hope that someday you get a bang out of a good contemporary service. The Phantom Avenger strikes again."

She knew better than to touch the note. Rafe Neilson has to see it in all its glory—except where the Avenger left it.

Maybe he'll admit that Lily's car wreck was anything but an accident.

SEVEN

Rafe was sitting in a dentist's chair early on Friday morning with a plastic suction wand hooked over his lip when Chief Porter's summons arrived in the form of a telephone call. Rafe flipped his cell phone open and mumbled, *"Yeth, Chieth."*

"I hate to foul up your visit to the dentist, but how soon can you get here?"

"I'll be there in twenty minuth, Chieth." He snapped the phone shut and glanced at the dental hygienist hovering over him. Because she wore a mask, all he could see of her face were two blue eyes behind a plastic safety shield. They had grown large—and looked more than a bit annoyed.

"You have fiftheen minuth," he said to her.

"I'll do my best." She poked at his gums with an instrument that looked like a miniature shepherd's crook.

"Outh!" he said.

"I can't hear you— I'm cleaning at maximum speed."

Twelve minutes later, Rafe ran his tongue over his squeaky-clean teeth. He had planned to eat breakfast after his visit to the dentist, but his mouth ached too much to even consider buying a breakfast sandwich at the Glorious Burger's drive-through window.

"Safety hint," he muttered as he walked to his Corvette. "Never get a dental hygienist ticked off at you."

I should have let her argue with the Chief.

Rafe drove across town—from Dock Street to Campbell Street—in less than ninety seconds. He had almost reached Police Headquarters when he noticed the dark red Volvo wagon parked in front.

Rats! My mouth feels like a bomb went off inside it, thanks to Emma McCall.

Well, he had encouraged her to take her complaints to Chief Porter. But he hadn't expected the Chief, a practical and sensible man, to take them seriously.

What in the world is going on?

He drove into the parking lot and backed the Corvette against the Deputy Chief sign. He noted that all of the building's windows and doors were closed, a sign that the stink-bomb residue had fully dissipated.

The Chief's office was behind the bull pen on the first floor. Rafe walked past two policemen sitting at their desks in the open area. They rolled their eyes; Rafe gave a helpless shrug in return. He reached the Chief's door, tapped gently on the center panel and turned the knob.

Chief Porter was behind his desk, wearing his "I'm unhappy about the circumstances" expression. And there *she* was—Emma McCall—sitting in one of the Chief's visitor chairs.

Rafe continued to push the door open…but stopped abruptly when he saw Tucker Mackenzie sitting in the chair next to her.

Why would Tucker and Emma be waiting for him in the Chief's office?

Chief Porter waved Rafe into the room.

"Good morning, Chief," Rafe said.

"Maybe not so good," he replied. "We've got a situation."

Rafe closed the door. The third chair in the Chief's office was a battered old ladder-back with a frayed caned seat that Gary Porter kept in a corner alongside an old metal file cabinet. Rafe moved it next to the Chief's desk so he would face both Emma and Tucker.

The Chief started talking the instant Rafe sat down.

"We—*you*—need to identify and arrest the so-called Phantom Avenger."

"Do we have a charge in mind?"

"Involuntary manslaughter."

The shock Rafe felt took his breath away.

"What?" he managed to say. "Who's the victim?"

"Lily Kirk." The Chief's voice sounded as if he had the full weight of the world on his shoulders.

Rafe strained to keep his voice calm. "Miss Kirk died in a routine traffic accident."

"No! She died because of this...." The Chief up-ended a small cardboard box, sending two plastic evidence bags skidding along the surface of his desktop toward Rafe.

He recognized the contents of the first bag immediately: the remains of an old ignition noisemaker, a practical joke that was popular during the 1950s and 1960s.

The Chief went on. "We're pretty sure that device was responsible for popping open the hood of the Taurus while Lily was barreling along State Road 34A. The results, as you know, were catastrophic."

Rafe picked up the second evidence bag and read the words neatly typed on a white file card: "'We hope that someday you get a bang out of a good contemporary service. The Phantom Avenger strikes again.'"

The Chief kept talking. "Ms. McCall and Tucker found both items last night in the engine compartment of Lily's car. I'll send them to the North Carolina State Bureau of Investigation for follow-up analysis. Maybe they can tell us more than we already know."

Rafe thought about asking how Emma McCall got permission to search beneath the hood of the wrecked Taurus, but why bother? He could imagine her following Tucker back to the Glory Garage and batting her long, dark eyelashes. Tucker was probably delighted to let her have a go at the old car.

You should have examined the inside of the engine compartment yourself.

Rafe picked up the bag containing the noisemaker. He studied it then glanced at Tucker. "Are you saying that this gadget exploded when Lily was driving on 34A?"

Tucker nodded, and then offered up an embarrassed grin. "That's evidently what happened, but I can't say why. The noisemaker should have gone off when she started the engine. Something delayed the blast."

"Maybe the NCSBI can help us figure that out, too," the Chief said. He seemed to hesitate before he added, "You know many of the young people who might be responsible for placing the device in the Taurus. I'm sorry, Rafe, but I intend to treat Lily's accident as a major crime."

Rafe felt a cold shiver crawl along his spine. The Chief was right. The Phantom Avenger would be held responsible for the prank gone bad. The "practical joke" had caused a death.

Emma rose to her feet. "Thank you, Chief Porter. I'm relieved to hear you say that."

Rafe avoided her gaze as she moved past him on her way to the door. Tucker Mackenzie followed her out of the office. Rafe felt his shoulders relax when he was alone with the Chief.

"What do you think?" Chief Porter said.

"The same thing you do. A delayed action noise-maker is like the stink bomb—a lot nastier than putting a car on a porch or dressing a statue. If high school kids are doing it, we've got a real problem in Glory."

The Chief nodded. "See what you can find out."

Rafe checked the wall clock in the bull pen as he left the police building. Ten thirty-five. He tried to remember Kate's schedule. If he hurried, her freshman cheerleading squad might still be practicing on the playing field. He put the Corvette in gear, roared out of the parking lot and headed east on Campbell then south on Broad. He used his cell phone to call Jessie Franklin, the principal.

"Hey, Jessie—it's Rafe Neilson."

"Hello, stranger."

"I know, I know. I owe you a visit."

"Not to mention lunch." She chuckled. "To what do I owe the honor of this call?"

"With your permission, I'd like to talk to my daughter, Kate. She should be practicing on the playing field."

"Her next class begins in ten minutes."

"I'll be finished in five."

"Okay, I'll alert the guards."

"You're a princess."

"And don't you forget it."

Rafe parked on the street and speed-walked to the back of the building. Two security guards were on duty. Rafe waved at them; they waved back.

He spotted Kate near the edge of the football field among a group of students who were practicing what looked like an exaggerated dance. Kate looked animated, bubbling over with laughter, a girl without a care in the world. He felt a cold finger of fear poke at his heart. She clearly held a leadership position in the Contemporaries.

"Please, God," he murmured, "don't let her be involved in Lily's death."

She saw him approaching. "Dad, what are you doing here?" Her smile vanished when she saw his expression. "What's wrong?"

He led her away from her friends to a quiet spot in the shadow of the bleacher seats. They should be able to talk there without being overheard.

"I'm going to ask you a couple of questions, Katy, and I need you to be completely honest with me. Okay?"

She nodded.

"No clever answers, no Fifth Amendment privileges."

"You're scaring me, Dad."

Rafe decided that it made no sense to sugarcoat the facts. Better to be blunt.

"You know that Lily Kirk was killed yesterday?" he said.

Kate nodded warily. "In a car accident, right?"

"Maybe not." He put his hands on her shoulders. "Kate, I'm going to tell you something you can't repeat to anyone. Okay?"

Her eyes grew wide as she nodded.

Rafe continued. "Lily Kirk's car was rigged with an ignition noisemaker—a big electrically operated fire-cracker that caused her hood to pop open. That's why she drove off the road." He let his words sink in. "Do you understand what that means?"

He saw Kate's face grow pale. "I think so," she said. "Was it a practical joke?"

"You tell me. We found a note signed by the Phantom Avenger."

"That's impossible!"

"Why?"

"Because we promised not to do things that go *bang*. I told you that. In fact, we decided to terminate the Phantom Avenger. We haven't done any pranks since last Tuesday." She began to cry. "We didn't set off the stink bomb, either—although I know you probably don't believe me."

He studied her face. The anguish looked real. As far as he knew, Katy had never lied to him. His instinct was to believe her.

"Who has the book of practical jokes?"

"I do, Dad. It's in my locker."

"You have five minutes to retrieve the book for me then get to your next class."

Katy turned then suddenly stopped. "Dad, will I need a lawyer?"

"Not if I can help it." He smiled. "Let's stop talking and start doing. Bring me the book."

"Okay, but you have to believe me. We didn't do it."

He watched Kate jog toward the school building. He wanted to believe her. There was no hard evidence, thank goodness, to link a student to the stink bomb or even the noisemaker—just two notes that could have been prepared by anyone.

The Chief knew that. He'd give the kids the benefit of the doubt. *But not Emma McCall.* The woman had an agenda. She wanted a town out of a Currier & Ives print—a town on its best behavior so that her B and B would prosper. Worse, her efforts at playing detective had paid off. Emma's initial success would probably motivate her to look for more rocks to turn over.

You can't let that happen.

There was only one way to keep her from becoming a wholly unpredictable loose cannon. He'd have to get close to her—make her think that she was part of *his* investigation.

Ouch. Without meaning to, he ground his teeth and made his gums ache.

She may be pretty, she may be smart, she may have long eyelashes—but you don't get paid enough to deal with the likes of Emma McCall.

Rafe stared at the yellow legal pad on his lap and drew a large question mark next to the words, *Lily Kirk's history.*

What did he know about Lily? Almost nothing—an odd fact when you consider that he'd been singing alongside her for more than three years. He had managed to write only three details on the pad: Lily served as the church's librarian, Lily was prominent in the Traditionalists, and Lily attended most church functions. He hadn't a clue about Lily's dreams, hopes, or concerns.

And now she was dead, killed in a freak automobile accident *possibly* caused by a practical joke. Emma McCall was sure of her deductions, but the North Carolina State Bureau of Investigation might reach another conclusion.

"Not very likely," Rafe muttered as he tried to get comfortable in the overstuffed wing chair. The Chief had talked about involuntary manslaughter, a serious crime in North Carolina, one that demanded a full investigation. Well, a good place to start any criminal investigation was to learn a little about the victim, and with Nina McEwen's help he would.

As if on cue, Nina stepped into her parlor carrying a tray laden with coffee and cookies. She set the tray on a low table in front of Rafe then sat down in a matching wing chair opposite his. He took a cup of black coffee but decided not to dull his shiny teeth with a cookie.

Rafe thoroughly enjoyed his contacts with Nina. He liked her as a person and coveted her skills as a choir director. He considered it extraordinary that a small church in a small town would have a member with her world-class credentials and experience.

"I apologize if I seem distracted," she said, "but I can't help feeling overwhelmed by the preparations for the funeral. There are so many last-minute details to worry about. And today I've begun to feel guilty that I feel overwhelmed. Lily Kirk was my oldest and dearest friend—" a frown crossed her face "—at least she was until recently. We used to have dinner together at least once each week and occasionally meet for breakfast. All of that stopped three weeks ago. I think she was mad at me for not siding with the Traditionalists."

Nina gazed up at the ceiling, clearly lost in thought. Rafe realized that she looked more tired than he had ever seen her before. After a while, she heaved another sigh and said, "Well, none of that makes any difference now that we're planning her funeral."

Rafe grunted. He knew that Nina had graciously taken charge of the arrangements for Lily Kirk's funeral on Friday afternoon because Lily had no spouse, no children and no living relatives that anyone knew of. In recent years, her church family had become her primary family.

"Unfortunately, Lily left no guidance of any kind," she said, "so that I have to make all the decisions about the casket, flowers, hymns, Scripture passages, invited guests, day, time—the list of small, but important, details goes on and on."

Rafe reached out and patted Nina's hand. He still remembered the challenge of planning a memorial service when his wife was killed. He wasn't surprised that Nina felt overwhelmed.

Nina finally returned his smile. "I'm okay. I just needed to complain a little to someone who would understand." She tugged at her skirt. "Now, what do you want me to tell you about Lily?"

"I want to understand her better," Rafe said. "I didn't get to know her in life as well as she deserved."

Nina stared into space a moment to gather her thoughts. When she began to speak, she spoke slowly and quietly. "If I could only use one word to describe Lily, I'd choose the word 'loner.' She was an only child who never married, a person who found it difficult to make friends. She seemed to enjoy being an eccentric who marched to the beat of her own drum."

"If memory serves, Lily hailed from Glory, like you."

"Indeed she did. Her father worked off and on at the Glory Hardware Store back when it was Glory Hardware and Feed."

"Off and on?"

Nina grimaced. "Len Kirk was a kind man, but he was addicted to gambling. He finally abandoned his family when Lily was seven or eight years old. That would have been in—" she peered at the opposite wall again "—in 1951. Lily's mother didn't feel able to raise Lily on her own, so she packed her off to her former husband's sister, a happily married woman with two other children who lived in Hoboken, New Jersey. That's where Lily grew up."

"Directly across the Hudson River from New York City."

"A hop, skip and jump away from Broadway— where the pair of us fell in love with musical comedies." Nina sighed. "You just reminded me—Lily's aunt passed a decade ago, but I'd better make sure that her cousins were notified about Lily's death.

Rafe let himself smile. "I'm astounded that you didn't lose touch with Lily."

"Well, we'd become fast friends in the first grade," Nina said. "It didn't take much to remain friends. The several weeks she spent with her mother each year, the letters we sent back and forth, plus our shared love of music, were enough. When I was sixteen, I began traveling to New Jersey during long school holidays to visit Lily. Bus fare was cheap back then. Naturally we saw as many Broadway shows as we could afford. We went mostly to Saturday matinees, which also didn't cost much during the late fifties."

Rafe nodded. He had decided to let Nina tell the story at her own pace, without any more prodding from him.

Nina kept talking. "Lily and I both graduated from high school in 1961. I went on to the University of North Carolina. Lily moved to Manhattan and found a job in a bookstore that specialized in used legal and medical books. Her dream, of course, was to become a star on Broadway."

Nina shrugged. "Lily never reached stardom, even though she had a lovely voice and could belt out a song with the best of them. Her problem was simple—she could sing, but she didn't have the acting and dancing skills a performer also needs to succeed in musical comedy."

"She was good—but not great," Rafe said softly.

"Like thousands of other hopefuls who fill the audition halls in New York City." Nina raised her right hand. "But let's not get too maudlin. In fact, Lily did sing in the chorus of several Broadway shows. I suppose the best known is *Bye Bye Birdie.* And she played small supporting roles in the national tours of *Annie Get Your Gun* and *Gypsy.*"

Nina let her hand fall back into her lap. "By the mid-1960s, though, Lily made peace with the fact that she'd never make it big on Broadway. She was luckier than some show-business wannabes. Her day job in the bookstore had given her a love for books and a good deal of specialized knowledge about them. She moved back to Glory in 1968 and became the town librarian."

"I assume that her mother was still alive when she came home?" Rafe said.

"Oh, yes. Emily Kirk didn't become seriously ill with Parkinson's disease until the late seventies. She died in 1985. Her long illness forced the sale of her home and consumed the modest savings that she and Lily had managed to put aside."

Rafe shook his head sadly. "That explains a lot. I'd guessed that Lily wasn't wealthy—now I know what she was up against. And yet, she never seemed gloomy about money."

"You're right. But Lily managed to hold on to a buoyant attitude despite her iffy finances. I didn't spend a lot of time with her, but I know that her faith helped a lot."

"Where were you living back then?"

"In Chapel Hill, North Carolina. I joined the music

faculty at the University of North Carolina in 1968, a few months after I earned my Doctor of Music degree at Indiana University." She gave a rueful smile. "It's only a four-hour drive from Chapel Hill to Glory. I should have visited Lily more often. After all, we'd been friends since we were five years old."

Rafe glanced at the pad on his lap. He wasn't happy about asking the next question, but it had to be asked. One remote possibility that no one had mentioned was that Lily had arranged "the accident" herself.

"Nina, Lily had good reason to become bitter during her life. Did she ever seem depressed or…"

Nina didn't wait for him to finish. "Or suicidal?" She shook her head. "Never! In fact, Lily kept her chorus-girl smile throughout her life."

"Her *what?*"

"Lily once told me that she'd learned to smile fetchingly during her chorus-girl days in New York. She claimed that the trick was to tilt your head to one side, show lots of teeth and fill your mind with cheerful thoughts. She often wore that smile—except perhaps during the past few weeks, when Lily seemed preoccupied by the recent events."

Rafe found it hard not to laugh. The librarian with the chorus-girl smile! He covered his amusement by asking, "Have you chosen the hymns we'll sing at Lily's funeral?"

He watched Nina's expression darken. "Not yet. 'Come Labor On' was one of Lily's favorites, but I can't make a final decision until I know who's going to sing at the funeral."

"I assumed that the whole choir will sing."

Nina looked down at her hands. "Frankly, I've been

hesitant to ask. With all the fighting going on, I'm worried that the Contemporaries might…"

Rafe waited for Nina to finish her sentence. When she didn't, he said, "That won't happen. No one in choir will refuse to sing at Lily's funeral tomorrow."

He saw tears at the corners of her eyes. "I'm not certain of that, Rafe. For the first time in my career, I've lost control of my singers. If this situation gets much worse…well, lots of people know that I've been thinking of resigning my post."

Rafe nodded slowly, not sure what else to do or say. Losing Nina McEwen would be an unimaginable disaster for the choir, but she was at the focal point of the squabbling in the church. The enmity would grow even worse if a prankster proved to be responsible for Lily's car wreck. And that was looking more and more the case.

"Thank you."

As he stood up, Nina said, "I've been praying that Lily's death will somehow reunite Glory Community Church. How wonderful it would be if Lily's tragic accident turns out to be the 'shock' that encourages both sides to stop fighting." She added, "Do you think that's too much to hope for?"

He smiled. "To tell the truth, Nina, I hope the very same thing."

EIGHT

Now what?

Emma looked at her reflection in the antique mirror in the Captain's first-floor hallway and wondered what she should—or could—do next that Friday morning. Her meeting with Chief Porter had gone well. He seemed to be taking Lily's death seriously. But was it merely a big show put on for her benefit? Would Glory's small-town police department really press forward with a genuine investigation? Emma could imagine the struggle going on in the Chief's mind.

On the one hand, an elderly woman died in an accident that was—as everyone knew—partially her fault. Had Lily Kirk not been speeding she might have been able to stop before she drove into the ditch. Moreover, had she been wearing her seat belt, she might have survived the crash anyway.

On the other hand, a bunch of local kids carried a practical joke too far. They hadn't set out to kill anyone. They were merely trying to make a point about church music. It would be unfair to charge them with involuntary manslaughter.

It's even more unfair that Lily is dead because of a foolish prank.

The telephone rang in Emma's office. She moved quickly to the small room next to the parlor and lifted the receiver.

"Good morning, Emma. It's Jackson Wallace. I'm organizing a special last-minute luncheon meeting of the Glory Chamber of Commerce. Half past noon today upstairs at The Glorious Table. Can I put you down as a yes?"

Emma ran through the list of things on her mental to-do list. "I'll be there." She added, "Why the special meeting?"

"We need to respond to the negative exposure Glory received on one of the Greenville TV stations last night. According to Channel Five, our town is overrun with teenage vandals who don't care who they hurt."

Rats!

Emma coughed to disguise the involuntary gasp she made. She had forgotten about Simon Rogers's promise to publicize the Phantom Avenger. What had he said to her? "This town is a grotesque hazard to life and limb." The man must have followed through on his threat.

Emma found it difficult to concentrate on business chores as Friday morning passed. The real possibility of a mountain of unflattering publicity represented one more reason why the Glory police might not want to delve too deeply into Lily Kirk's "accident."

Be honest. You're terrified of bad press, too.

All the businesses in Glory, including The Scottish Captain, would suffer if tourists thought of Glory as a town full of out-of-control teenagers. The truth of Lily's car wreck would trigger a whole new round of stories about Glory's "vicious Phantom Avenger."

We can't brush Lily's death under the rug.

Emma heard herself sigh. There had to be a middle ground, an approach that would punish the person responsible for killing Lily without destroying Glory.

But where is it?

She felt relieved when it was time to walk over to The Glorious Table.

Emma had first seen the Table's fancy antiqued parchment menu a week after she moved to town. The cute plaid ribbon, the faux-Scottish dish names—including Trout Loch Lomond and Mary Queen of Scots Tournedos—and the steep prices had set off her innkeeper alarm bells. She had dined at too many phony posh eateries that worked harder at being flamboyant than at serving well-prepared food.

Emma had changed her mind when she attended her first monthly gathering of the Glory Chamber of Commerce. By the end of lunch, Emma agreed that the Table was Glory's finest eatery and among the best restaurants in North Carolina.

The dish that prompted Emma's about-face was Isle of Skye Chicken Salad—an oddly named but fabulously delicious concoction of chicken, mayonnaise, curry powder, bits of vegetables and nuts, plus a secret ingredient or two she hadn't been able to figure out. Emma invariably ordered chicken salad at Chamber meetings, and today's special meeting would be no exception.

The Glorious Table occupied an imposing nineteenth century house at the corner of King Street and Stuart Lane, a pleasant three-block walk from The Scottish Captain. The owners had converted the whole second

floor into a private dining room that could accommodate fifty people. Accordingly, the Chamber and most
other civic organizations in Glory held their meetings
at the Table.

Emma liked the feel of the place. The walls throughout the building were covered with elegant textured
wallpaper—a mostly yellow-and-red pattern that immediately signaled the restaurant's Scottish theme. Framed
paintings of Scotsmen in kilts dotted the walls. Scattered among them were bagpipes hung as ornaments
and photos of the castles associated with different
Scottish clans.

Emma knew that the restaurant reviewer from
Southern Life magazine had criticized the surfeit of
Gaelic decor as "off-putting to one's appetite." Well, he
might as well have complained about red, white and
blue bunting in Washington, DC. Glory, after all, had
been founded by Scots. In 1731, a contingent of Scottish
wool merchants emigrated from Scotland and spent
their first winter near Cape Fear, North Carolina. They
subsequently took advantage of a generous land grant
provided by Governor Gabriel Johnston—a fellow
Scot—and moved inland, to the western side of the
Albemarle Sound. They laid out the boundaries of
Glory in the spring of 1733 and established a local wool
processing industry. The original settlers were later
joined by other Scottish émigrés, attracted by Glory's
growth and prosperity.

Emma climbed the stairs that led to the second floor,
slowing down to look, as she usually did, at the row of
small wooden wall plaques that displayed the tartans of
different Scottish clans. She stopped a moment at Clan
McCall, a predominantly red-and-green pattern with

thin black-and-white lines, that would make excellent Christmas wrapping paper. As always, she chuckled at the thought.

She counted about twenty people in the Lochinvar Room, sitting in small groups at five round tables, each one large enough to hold ten diners. She looked for a friendly face.

"Emma! Sit with us at the B and B table."

Emma spotted Carol Dorsey waving at her. She was with her husband, Bill, at the table to the right of the entrance arch. Sitting across from the Dorseys were Dave and Ellen Stein.

Emma returned their smiles and made her way to the table, as always finding it difficult to tell the two pairs of B and B keepers apart. Carol Dorsey was a lanky blonde just shy of fifty; Bill was midfiftyish and well fed, with thick salt-and-pepper hair. They owned The Robert Burns Inn on Campbell Street. The Steins, proprietors of Glory House on Front Street, matched the Dorseys in every key particular. Carol and Ellen might have been cousins; Dave and Bill seemed more like brothers.

"Hi-ho, Emma," Dave Stein said. "How be thee?"

"I don't have a care in the world," Emma fibbed.

"Lucky you. We've been so busy that I could use a vacation."

Ellen Stein made a disparaging gesture. "Give me a break! You'd want to go to another B and B and spend the whole day taking notes and wondering if the owner does things better than we do."

Emma stopped to let portly Jackson Wallace—who had muttered a loud "Excuse me, Emma"—maneuver past her to reach the table closest to a large bay window that overlooked Stuart Lane. Chamber tradition decreed that this was the head table and that Jackson, who had been president of the Glory Chamber of Commerce for the past decade, lead each meeting from that location. Jackson owned The Glory Gifter, the somewhat tacky gift and souvenir shop on Main Street. He had lived in Glory his whole life; his ancestors had arrived in town before the Civil War.

Jackson had visited Emma three days after she'd moved into the Captain and had practically ordered her to sign up. "Every businessperson in town is a member of our Chamber of Commerce," he had said, "including all of the B and B owners. They'll expect to see you at the next monthly meeting." In fact, he had been right; Chamber membership seemed to go hand and hand with owning a business in Glory.

The precise kind of business didn't seem to make any difference to Jackson. He had even managed to convince Sara Knolls to join the Chamber. Emma couldn't fathom why a writer of do-it-yourself books would care about local business issues—but there Sara was, sitting at an adjacent table chatting animatedly with Tony Taylor, the owner of Glory at Sea marina.

Emma chose a vacant chair between the Dorseys and the Steins. Carol Dorsey peered at her. "Are you sure you're okay? You don't look carefree."

"I guess I'm still reeling from Lily Kirk's death."

"A tragedy, pure and simple," Bill Dorsey said. "An *inevitable* tragedy. Lily loved to put her pedal to the metal. Her sins finally caught up with her."

"I suppose so," Emma said vaguely. "Pedal to the metal" was fast becoming a mantra to explain Lily's accident. Emma wondered if she should set people straight and explain that fast driving alone had not killed

Lily. No one had asked her not to talk about the ignition noisemaker, but…

Better not spread the details around. Not yet.

Emma changed the subject. "Who's going to Lily's funeral?"

"I will," Ellen Stein said, "but Dave won't. Both of us can't be gone from The Glory House at the same time on a Friday afternoon. Even this luncheon meeting is a stretch for us."

Emma and the Dorseys nodded together. The Glory House was the most expensive B and B in town and tended to attract a fussy, highly demanding clientele who expected "staff" to be on duty twenty-four hours a day.

A new voice joined in. "Lily Kirk deserves more respect than your spoiled customers."

Emma looked up. Sam Lange had moved next to an empty chair. "Mind if I sit with you folks?" he asked.

"Please do, Sam," Bill Dorsey replied. "We prefer to think of our guests as demanding rather than fussy."

Sam dropped into the chair. "Fine with me. *Demanding* is a synonym for *royal pain*." He smiled broadly then said, "I'm closing my shop all day Friday in honor of Lily. She was the best librarian Glory ever had. A real whiz about books."

Emma abruptly remembered the books scattered around Lily's wrecked car. "I visited the accident scene," she said. "The trunk of Lily's car had been full of books that belonged to you."

"My weekly shipment of worthless old books from John Caruthers's attic. A cop car brought some of them to my shop. I picked up the rest at The Glory Garage. They'll make great kindling for my fireplace this winter." He gave Emma a military salute. "Thanks for thinking of me."

When Emma lifted her hand to return the salute, a cool, bony hand gripped her fingers.

"I wanted to tell you again," a wobbly voice said, "how thrilled I am that someone like yourself has taken over The Scottish Captain. We all feared that the place would be bought by hippies."

Emma smiled over her shoulder at Ethel Dowling, the aged and somewhat forgetful mother of Miriam Dowling, the owner of The Glorious Table.

"Many of my customers are former hippies, Ethel."

"Really? With flowers in their hair and Volkswagen vans?"

"Mostly with pearl necklaces, diamond earrings and BMW sedans. Those hippies of old are today's solid citizens."

"That's nice, dear." Ethel released her grip on Emma's hand and moved off to visit another table.

"Hippies?" Dave said when Ethel was out of earshot. "I haven't heard that word in decades."

"The woman is crazy as a loon," Sam said. "She shouldn't be walking around without supervision."

Carol laughed. "Ethel's a kind soul, but forty years behind the times."

"Here come the waiters and waitresses," Bill said.

"Wunderbar!" Dave said, "I'm getting hungry."

Emma tugged her chair closer to the table as the waitstaff strode into the dining room. They were an efficient bunch and took luncheon orders in less than three minutes from the forty-odd people now in the room. Emma needed less than ten seconds to place her order: "Chicken salad platter. Ranch dressing on the side."

"Let's start our meeting while we're waiting for our food to arrive." Jackson's voice made the room quake.

Emma recoiled as she always did when he made a booming announcement. The man didn't need a sound system to be heard, but he liked to use one.

He continued, "First things first. Because this is a special meeting, we need God's help today more than ever. I've invited Daniel Hartman, senior pastor of Glory Community Church, to offer an invocation."

He was at a table across the room surrounded by people Emma didn't know. One of the paradoxical challenges of living in a small, friendly town was that no one wore name tags at meetings, on the assumption that everyone knew everyone else. But because the locals didn't wear name tags, it was difficult to get to know them.

Emma hadn't noticed Daniel come in, nor was she aware that he'd been tapped to lead the group in prayer. Jackson never explained how he chose his pastors du jour, but his selection of Daniel seemed especially appropriate. The "mess" began in Glory Community's choir loft. Who better to pray for an end to the conflict?

"Go, Daniel!" Sam said, loudly enough to make Emma cringe. She hoped that Daniel, some thirty feet away, hadn't been embarrassed by Sam's silly "encouragement."

"Ladies and gentlemen," Daniel said. "Please join with me in a prayer."

Emma bowed her head and tried to drive the morning's worries from her mind.

"Heavenly Father," Daniel began. "We are thankful for all that You have given us, including the strength to deal with the trials that have beset Glory in recent days. This is a time of testing for us—a time of problems born of strife *inside* the Body of Christ.

"Christians have bickered and fought and shattered the unity of Your church throughout the past two millennia. We gather today to examine the fruit of this foolishness—to repair the unnecessary injuries that our prideful conduct has caused.

"We ask for the discernment to better understand our tribulations, the wisdom to choose the right courses of action and the courage to forgive those who *seem* to be our enemies, but are really our brothers and sisters in Christ.

"Lastly Father, we give thanks for the food we will receive today, for the cooks who cooked it, for the people who serve our meals and for the many bounties that You pour out on us every day. In our Savior's name, Amen."

Emma added her "Amen" to the chorus and opened her eyes.

Jackson Wallace tapped his microphone. "Thank you, Daniel." Jackson paused to collect his thoughts before he said, "The purpose of this special meeting is to discuss our response to the…uh…*outrageous and inflammatory* news report that aired on Channel Five last night. We've ordered both a DVD and a transcript of the segment, but we can't wait until they arrive to take action.

"For those who didn't see the story, Glory's Phantom Avenger was thoroughly discussed on the eleven o'clock news. The piece was a full three minutes long. A New England travel writer by the name of Simon Rogers was the focal point, but the report also included sound bites by Glory's own Nina McEwen, Chief Porter and Rex Grainger.

"Nina summarized the conflict at Glory Community Church, the Chief labeled the pranks a cry for attention, and Rex—who should have known better—waxed poetic about how the decline of moral values in Glory led inevitably to the Phantom Avenger and the dwindling of our property rights."

Emma looked around the dining room as several Chamber members issued boos and catcalls. Rex, a long-term member of the Chamber, had wisely stayed away from this meeting. Sam Lange muttered, "Our local newspaperman is a blithering idiot."

Jackson Wallace gestured for quiet. "However, nothing Rex said had one-tenth the impact of Simon Rogers's on-air tirade. He repeatedly used the word *hooliganism* to describe the recent antics of Glory's teenagers.

"Moreover, I learned this morning that an equally vituperative article about Glory appeared in this morning's edition of the *Daily Herald* in Portland, Maine."

Emma felt like sliding under the table as the members produced a new and even louder gust of boos and hisses. Simon Rogers had been her guest. Had she really done everything possible to calm him down on the afternoon he fled Glory?

Jackson continued. "Naturally, I've asked Channel Five and the *Daily Herald* for equal time. They have agreed to do follow-up reports on Glory—which should help undo some of the damage that Rogers did. But—" Jackson breathed a deep sigh "—frankly, I'm bewildered by the man's hostility to us. He advised travelers to avoid Glory unless Edenton and Elizabeth City are in ruins. He seemed especially incensed over the stink bomb that shut down our police building. In fact, he made it sound like a personal attack against him."

Emma raised her hand. "Jackson, I can shed some light on his reactions."

She stood up. Several members passed a handheld

microphone across the line of tables. She cleared her throat and said, "Simon Rogers was a guest…"

"We can't hear you," a man at the head table shouted.

"Turn the microphone on," called a woman across the room.

"Uh…how do I do that?" Emma peered at the microphone's handle. There must be a switch, but where was it?

Sara Knoll bounded out of her chair, moved to Emma's side and studied the microphone for a few seconds. "I thought so!" She gave the bottom of the handle a clockwise twist. The next words she spoke— "It switches on like some flashlights"—reverberated through the dining room.

"Three cheers for Glory's own Martha," Jackson said.

Emma accepted the microphone from Sara and began again. "Simon Rogers was a guest at The Scottish Captain during his visit to Glory. He was enchanted by the sight of the Volkswagen Beetle convertible on my porch. He even helped to ease my fears on the morning it happened. I worried that the car might cave in my porch— He assured me that a well-built structure could easily handle the extra weight.

"He thought the other practical jokes were funny, too—the relocated fish, the dressed statue, the phony parking ticket on Chief Porter's car.

"His opinion flip-flopped, though, when the Phantom Avenger targeted Police Headquarters. Simon was inside the building when the stink bomb exploded. He believed that he needed medical care…"

"For what?" a woman at a distant table said.

Emma looked toward the woman and shrugged. "Simon claimed he was allergic to the chemical compounds that contain sulfur. He did smell like a rotten egg when he returned to the Captain."

Sam Lange shouted, "What else do you expect a skunk to smell like?"

Emma went on when the laughter subsided. "There's no doubt that Simon overreacted. However, his behavior confirms the old truism that one's view of a practical joke depends greatly on the choice of 'victim.' I might have found the Volkswagen episode more entertaining if the Bug had ended up on someone else's porch. And Simon would have left Glory a happy travel reporter if he had not had the misfortune to visit the police department."

Jackson Wallace took charge again. "Thank you, Emma! *Overreact* seems the perfect word to describe Simon Rogers. He has done his readers and viewers a disservice. The Phantom Avenger aimed his pranks at townsfolk. They never represented a threat to visitors."

"You're right," a man at the head table said. "I saw the interview. He made it sound like the Phantom Avenger killed someone."

Emma's heart skipped as she took a step backward, bumped into her chair and nearly dropped the microphone. The loud *thump* echoed between the walls of the dining room.

Jackson nodded vigorously. "You're right! Visitors from Europe and Asia are exceptionally sensitive to reports of violence directed at tourists. Rogers's deceptive reporting will cause us problems for months to come."

Emma glanced to her left and her right. No one seemed to have noticed her odd burst of activity. She passed the mic back to Jackson and sat down.

The discussion took off as people at every table began to participate:

"Can someone tell me what *hooliganism* means? I haven't used it for years and I've forgotten."

"A hooligan is a thug."

"Well, if we stick with that definition, there's no hooliganism in Glory. Just kids playing practical jokes."

"Yeah, but you heard Emma. One man's prank can be another man's hooliganism. It's all about perception. Perception is reality."

"Rogers was a terrible tipper. We served him two meals at Snacks of Glory. He left both times without tipping."

"You can't trust a man who doesn't leave a tip. It's a symptom of a flawed character."

"Simon Rogers has shoveled his dirt. He's not the issue anymore. We need new and better ways to dig ourselves out and attract tourists to Glory."

"How about discount accommodation packages that include B and Bs, restaurant meals and local attractions—all at one discount price?"

"How much of a discount? I don't want to lose money."

"Let's take advantage of Glory's Scottish heritage. We can link ourselves to a sister city in Scotland. That might increase the number of tourists from Great Britain."

"I have a better idea. Ghosts are very popular. Let's set up a walking tour through Glory's haunted houses."

"That would be a short walk. We don't have any notable ghosts living in Glory."

"I move that we make Simon Rogers our official town ghost and put him to work as soon as possible."

"We may not have ghosts, but Glory is chock-full of secret compartments and assorted hidey-holes."

"That's true. I've heard that every house built before 1910 had one."

"You bet! Our Scottish forebears came from an area

of Scotland noted for smuggling. They needed a place to hide contraband goods."

"The *real* story is more interesting. Back in the nineteenth century, Glory didn't have a local bank because the citizenry didn't trust banks. Secret compartments served as an alternative way to protect one's valuables and money. If thieves couldn't find your nest egg, they couldn't steal it."

"Don't forget that Sara Knolls is a bona fide expert on secret compartments. She wrote two articles on the subject."

"That hardly makes me an *expert,* but I do know a lot about the subject and I would be happy to write the text for a brochure that we can give to tourists."

"Great! We'll have hidey-hole tours. Visitors can tap our walls, peer into fireplaces, look behind mirrors and paintings. The people who find hiding places get prizes."

"Trouble is, lots of us don't know where our hidey-holes are. How about you, Emma?"

Emma needed a few seconds to realize that Ellen Stein had spoken to her.

"Pardon?" Emma said.

"Everyone knows that The Scottish Captain has a secret compartment that was used as a money safe during the nineteenth Century."

"Really? Where is it?" Emma asked.

"Ah! There's the rub. No one alive today knows. Carole and Duncan Frasier searched for years and never found it. They finally concluded that it doesn't exist."

"But you think it does?"

Ellen smiled. "Most every nineteenth century house had one."

Dave Stein leaned toward Emma and said, "Don't

believe anything that Ellen tells you about hidey-holes. She is an incurable romantic, who—"

A loud *thunk* interrupted Dave in midsentence. Emma glanced at the head table in time to see Jackson Wallace rap his microphone again. "Our food has arrived. As we enjoy our lunches, let's think about what we can do to restore Glory's reputation. We'll return to our discussion during dessert."

Emma shifted in her chair so the waitress could place the chicken-salad platter in front of her. The immediate need, she decided, wasn't to restore Glory's reputation. A more pressing problem was to prevent further deterioration.

We can't let the world know that Lily Kirk's death wasn't an accident. At least, not yet.

She scooped up a forkful of chicken salad. It tasted as good as she'd anticipated.

But how do I convince Rafe Neilson to run a discreet investigation that leads to a quiet conclusion?

NINE

Daniel paused at the door to the sanctuary to listen to the murmur of voices inside. No shouts. No insults. No vocal duels.

Praise God! They're not fighting. Perhaps Saturday is a day of cease-fire in Glory.

Daniel thought about his own shortcomings. *And, Lord…please help me keep my temper in check.*

Much to his chagrin, he'd flown into a rage on Friday afternoon after Lily's funeral when he'd read the letter signed by the "seven surviving Traditionalists," as they'd called themselves. Happily, no one else had seen the pastor kick his wastebasket across the room. Or smash a lovely glass paperweight, handmade in Germany, that he'd owned for twenty years.

The cause of his fury had been the letter's crescendo:

We have no doubt that the stress of the situation caused by those singers who favor the contemporary service was largely responsible for the death of Lily Kirk. We find it impossible to continue standing next to them during future worship services. We will participate with them at Lily Kirk's funeral service today, but we expect you and Dr. McEwen to resolve the matter one way or another.

In other words, choose us or choose them.

The sheer gall of the demand had infuriated Daniel. *How dare they issue an ultimatum that will devastate Nina McEwen?* He couldn't remember another time he had been as angry. Not even the grim experience of pastoring during war had triggered as intense an emotional reaction.

Daniel had regained his composure by late Friday afternoon. He spent two hours after Lily's funeral calmly and coolly arranging a special meeting of the choir on Saturday morning—not taking no for an answer if anyone offered an excuse for not attending.

If he could "waste" a beautiful Saturday morning, so could they. He had planned to spend the day surf fishing on the Outer Banks. It was only a two hour drive from Glory to Corolla, North Carolina. There were few recreations he considered more relaxing than standing in the surf and casting for bluefish.

But the fish would have to wait until he had done his best to restore peace at Glory Community Church. That's what the Elder Board expected him to do, but Daniel wasn't confident that the singers would listen to him or that he could get the two factions to talk to one another. He did, however, feel certain that this noisy, messy dispute would rip the congregation apart if he couldn't stop it.

Daniel paused near the door to the sanctuary and unfolded a sheet of paper. He had asked Nina McEwen to provide a tabular "map" of the choir to help him remember the singers' names, vocal parts and relationship to the dispute. On her own, she had included oc-

cupations and "guesstimates" of their ages on the theory
that more information about them might help Daniel
communicate more effectively.

Phoebe Hecht Soprano Physician 50+	Michelle Engle Soprano Housewife About 35	Emma McCall Soprano Owns B&B Under 35	Lane Johnson Baritone Postmaster Fiftyish	Tony Taylor Baritone Owns marina 55+	Rafe Neilson Baritone Deputy Chief Under 40
Debbie Akers Soprano H.S. Student 17	Judy Vines Alto Waitress 25+	Candy Cole Alto Housewife Fiftyish	Jake Moore Tenor H.S. Student 17	Sam Lange Tenor Runs bookstore 55+	Larry Borstahl Baritone Hardware Store About 45
Jacqui Naismith Alto Retired teacher 70+	Becky Taylor Alto Chief nurse Fiftyish			Dave Early Tenor Runs gas station Fiftyish	Rich. Squires Tenor Owns restaurant Sixtyish

Nina had identified the choir's seven Contemporaries with light gray shading and left the seven surviving Traditionalists clear. She included Jake Moore in the former group; he had acknowledged his true colors during the previous week. Finally, she highlighted the two uncommitted singers—Emma and Rafe—with dark shading.

As Daniel studied the choir map, he noticed two things. First, Nina had made a small change in the singers' placements to compensate for the absence of Lily Kirk. Debbie Akers used to stand directly in front of Candy Cole and Lily in front of Phoebe Hecht. Second, the sixteen singers represented an eclectic group: a broad spectrum of ages and a variety of different occupations.

Daniel ignored the knot in his stomach and pushed open the door. The sight he saw in the sanctuary might have been funny if the situation wasn't so serious. The Contemporaries sat near the back of the room on the right side of the center aisle; the Traditionalists had arrayed

themselves on the left. The two undeclared singers—Rafe
Neilson and Emma McCall—proclaimed their in-
between status by sitting up front in the sanctuary, close
to the aisle.

*Well, at least the mess can't get any worse than it
is right now.*

Emma watched and listened as Daniel strode down
the aisle to the pastor's lectern. The boots he had chosen
to wear this morning made an especially loud clomp that
stopped the murmuring conversations in the pews instantly. For a moment she imagined Daniel taking
charge of a company of army troops, then remembered
he had been an army chaplain, not a combat commander.

"Thank you for participating today, ladies and gentlemen," Daniel said without preamble or smile. "I
intend to offer a prayer, but before I do I want to explain
two simple facts of life to everyone here today."

Emma guessed that Daniel might have had some theatrical training. He'd paused at the perfect time to heighten
the dramatic effect, used the few moments of silence to
scan both groups of singers and cleverly adjusted his expression to match the tone of his voice: a mixture of anger,
determination and absolute unwillingness to compromise.

Emma considered asking Rafe what he thought of
Daniel's "performance," but decided not to. This was a bad
time for whispered conversations and, anyway, Rafe might
not feel comfortable analyzing what the pastor had done.

Daniel finally continued. "First, quitting is not an
option. No singer will leave the choir in response to Lily
Kirk's death or the recent actions of the so-called Contemporaries. Is that understood?"

Daniel paused again. When none of the singers

responded, he repeated his question—significantly louder this time.

"Is that understood?"

Emma glanced around the sanctuary as heads began to nod. Several people mumbled soft yesses.

"Good. Second—there will be no more shouting matches or fistfights or wrestling matches at choir meetings. Is that understood?"

More nods. More softly spoken yesses.

All at once, Emma understood Daniel's strategy. He wanted to keep the choir members confused and docile, focused on him rather than each other. She thought back to the courses she had taken on dispute resolution and mediation—two techniques that she'd often applied when resolving personnel issues at the Pacific Monarch Hotel. Daniel was clearly trying to move the choir safely out of the minefield of explosive emotions that threatened Glory Community Church. The first step was to remind the choir members that he, not the choir, was in charge. He seemed to have succeeded.

"Let us pray," Daniel said. He extended both hands, palms upward, in the manner of an Old Testament priest. "Dear Lord, we come before You as sinful and broken people who ask You to forgive our sins. We know that You will forgive us in the same measure as we forgive those who have hurt us. We ask You to accept our prayers of regret for the wrong things we have done and for the necessary things we've left undone. We forgive those who have hurt us and we will strive to remember that we are all Your children, no matter how we pray, or how we worship, or what songs we sing.

"All that we do during worship is meant to be a sweet

fragrance to You, Lord. Be with us this morning as we seek to repair the rift in Your church.

"In Jesus's name we pray, Amen."

Emma heard several of the singers sitting near her add their own Amens.

"Good!" Daniel slowly scanned the choir, then took a deep breath. "My friends, I can't help but notice that you have chosen seats that reflect your worship style biases. Consequently, the first thing we'll do this morning is play musical pews. I want the choir sitting in the first three pews directly in front of me. Please arrange yourself according to the pattern of vocal parts that Dr. McEwen designed."

Emma looked to her left and right and saw several faces register puzzlement.

"It's a simple request," he said. "Reconstitute the choir in front of me—sopranos, altos, tenors and baritones in an approximation of your usual positions. Emma McCall and Rafe Neilson stay where you are—the rest of you find seats around them."

Daniel seemed to work hard to maintain an inscrutable expression as the singers moved—without much enthusiasm, Emma thought—to the front of the sanctuary.

Emma kept looking forward until the shuffling noises stopped, then she glanced at the pews. Only two of the "combatants"—Lane Johnson and Tony Taylor—appeared unhappy to be sitting side by side. The other singers seemed more curious to learn what Daniel intended to do next.

Daniel gripped the lectern with both hands and leaned forward in what Emma read as an aggressive pose. "My first objective this morning," he said, "is to fully understand the motivation behind the schism we see in our congregation. Is there anyone in the choir who actively seeks the destruction of Glory Community Church?"

Emma counted five "no's" and one "of course not!" She noted that many of the singers had averted their eyes in what seemed to be embarrassment.

"Good," Daniel went on. "I expected that question to make you feel uncomfortable. Well, that leaves us with a rather awkward situation. We have a nasty fight that threatens to destroy the church going on among people who support Glory Community and presumably want it to prosper. Am I right?"

Emma spoke a soft, "You are." She heard several sighs, some foot shuffling and a few hesitantly spoken "yesses." Rafe said nothing. She glanced at him; he seemed lost in thought.

"Okay…" Daniel softened his voice. "Is any member of the choir willing to articulate the position held by those who want the Caruthers inheritance to be spent on our contemporary service? A brief explanation will be useful for all of us."

Emma wondered who in the choir would accept Daniel's challenge. The Contemporaries best spokesperson, she thought, was Tony Taylor, a man with navy command experience. He should be able to deftly summarize their position.

To Emma's surprise, Debbie Akers, a junior at Glory High School, stood up. "Pastor," she said, "contemporary worship is where it's at. Look at the largest and fastest-growing churches in America. They all have contemporary services. Younger people overwhelmingly prefer praise music to traditional hymns, and so do most 'seekers' who haven't committed to becoming Christians. We need a first-class contemporary service to help our church grow and to support our evangelism and disciple-making programs. We probably also need a good traditional worship service for those who prefer one. But it seems wrong to invest money in a pipe organ to support a worship format that is becoming less and less popular. Once we install a humongous pipe organ, we'll never be able to have a good contemporary service again, because the organ pipes and console will fill half the available space in the front of the church."

Debbie nodded at Judy Vines and Rebecca Taylor, the two Contemporaries nearest her, and then sat down.

Daniel smiled and said, "Thank you, Debbie, for your forthright statement. Now, is anyone willing to present the position of those who want the Caruthers money to go to our traditional service?"

Emma saw a hand shoot up on her right. Larry Borstahl, the owner of Glory Hardware & Feed on King Street, rose to his feet.

"Fifty years from now," Larry said, "the traditional church service might be as rare as the traditional hardware store has become. Today, however, the majority of members of Glory Community Church attend traditional worship. We may be old-fashioned, out of step and doomed to extinction, but we're also the people who pay for this church. I include John Caruthers in that 'we.' John was a member of the choir. He tithed to this church, and he loved traditional worship music." Larry made a sweeping gesture. "The fundamental disagreement we have with the Contemporaries is that we refuse to allow this sanctuary to become a rock concert venue. They want to eliminate the pews, transform the dais into a performance stage, move the table we use for the Lord's Supper to the side and install lighting and sound systems big enough for a football stadium. That's a tad more change than we're willing to accept in one installment."

The moment Larry finished, Lane Johnson and Richard Squires began to applaud.

Daniel rapped his lectern with his knuckles. "I should have explained," he said loudly, "that I will not allow partisan cheerleading today. We already know which side each of us prefers. Our goal is to fully understand the differing positions. Specifically, do they represent two mutually exclusive points of view that can lead to only one winner?"

Emma thought about the two opposing statements she'd just heard. They'd both been self-serving, but they'd also seemed poles apart. It would take a miracle to achieve a compromise between the Contemporaries and the Traditionalists.

"Where do you stand on the issue, Pastor?" asked Jacqueline Naismith, a large woman with a larger voice.

Daniel shook his head. "I won't give you a direct answer, Jacqui. The last thing our congregation needs is for me to come down on one side or another. That will guarantee a fatal split." He took a breath. "I'll give you the same answer I gave to the committee that will recommend how the church spends the Caruthers bequest. I'll share my preference after the decision is made. Pastors come and go, but a pipe organ or a performance stage will be with the church for decades to come. It must be the church's decision—and yours alone." He paused a moment. "Now, let's have another round of opinions."

Emma wondered if Daniel was right not to steer the

congregation. Sometimes a good mediator had to "encourage" movement toward a compromise position.

Especially when the opponents are as entrenched as these two groups.

It occurred to Rafe as he followed the other choir members out of the sanctuary that Lily Kirk's funeral would probably be less gloomy than the special choir meeting he had just attended.

Rafe could read Daniel Hartman's growing frustration on his face; his eyes looked tired and his gaunt cheeks proclaimed a recent loss of weight. Rafe certainly didn't envy Daniel's responsibilities. Pastoring a squabbling congregation looked as tough a job as he could imagine.

Was it even possible to heal the breach? Maybe the best solution would be to divide Glory Community in two—create a traditional church and a contemporary church and split the Caruthers money among the two halves. That at least would put an end the bickering and also further pranks.

Debbie Akers had stopped in the narthex to chat with Jake Moore. Although Rafe didn't want to believe it, it was possible that this pair of young Contemporaries had been malicious enough to place the ignition noisemaker in Lily Kirk's car.

No. That would mean Kate was probably involved.

Rafe drove the thought from his mind. An obvious question immediately took its place.

If the kids didn't do it, who did?

He needed to find out *quickly.*

He also had to "defuse" Emma McCall before she did any more unauthorized investigating. He had hoped to visit her on Friday, but he had spent much of the day dealing with an investigator and an evidence technician from the North Carolina State Bureau of Investigation.

He spotted Emma leaving through the front door. He jogged after her and caught up on King Street. "Are you bound for The Scottish Captain?" he asked.

She stopped immediately. "The very place."

"Can I talk you into a brief detour for a cup of coffee? I'd like to chat with you."

"I'm up for coffee. As it happens, I'd like to chat with you, too. Do you have a place in mind?"

"How about Snacks of Glory, across from Founders Park?"

"Fine with me." She smiled courteously. "But I insist we go dutch treat."

Rafe struggled to hide his astonishment. He had offered to buy her a cup of coffee. Nothing more. But if he accidentally offended her, she'd probably leave him standing alone on King Street.

"Dutch treat it is," he said.

They about-faced and retraced their steps past Glory Community Church. Rafe felt curiously pleased—there was no other word to describe the feeling—as he walked alongside Emma. He even was tempted to take her arm.

She'll laugh at you if you try.

He glanced sideways at her for an instant. It's nothing but a routine chemical reaction, he concluded, brought on by the fact that Emma looks remarkably pretty this morning.

It must be the way the sunlight strikes her face.

He cleared his throat. "What did you think of our special choir meeting?"

"You know that I'm not a member of Glory Community Church. You also know that I want to steer clear of the dispute. I tried to explain all that to Daniel when he called me yesterday, but he kept insisting that I attend this morning." She threw up her hands. "In the end, I couldn't say no to him."

Rafe uttered a noncommittal "uh-huh." She hadn't answered his question, but it would be risky to press her further. He enjoyed the companionable silence as they walked east on Oliver Street.

"Here we are," he said, when they reached Snacks of Glory, directly across the street from the entrance to Founders Park. The smell of renowned "SOG-gy Burgers" wafting through the air reminded Rafe that he hadn't eaten breakfast this morning. Perhaps he would order something more substantial than coffee.

"I need some solid food to accompany my coffee," he said. "How about you?"

She smiled. "I'm suddenly in the mood for comfort food, too."

Rafe stood behind her as Emma ordered—and paid for herself—a SOG-gy Burger with all the trimmings and a double cappuccino. He ordered a SOG-gy Burger— "hold the onions"—a regular coffee and a caramel apple.

"I haven't eaten a caramel apple since I was a kid," she said.

"It's my compensation for sitting through that awful meeting."

Her smile faded. "I hate to talk about the dissension at the church because I find the whole situation terribly depressing. I know what Daniel is trying to do. I took a course on mediation back in college, but I'm not sure he can pull it off. The choir and the congregation may be too polarized to reach a compromise."

Rafe nodded. "That's what I think, too. Neither side

seems ready to acknowledge a middle ground, a place where reasonable people can agree."

He spotted an empty table for two. "Shall we?"

"Let's, but no more small talk. We didn't come here to discuss Glory Community."

"True enough. Who goes first?"

"The policeman, of course," she said, with a laugh.

Rafe pulled out Emma's chair; they made themselves comfortable at the small table.

"You did a nifty piece of detective work the other day when you found the noisemaker in Lily's car," he said. "You deserve to know where it's taking us."

Rafe waited to see Emma's reaction to his compliment. She took a small bite of her burger and looked at him with an expression that seemed more doubtful than pleased.

Okay…from now on, just the facts, ma'am.

Rafe continued, "An evidence technician from the North Carolina State Bureau of Investigation examined Lily's car yesterday and took the remains of the noisemaker back to Raleigh for analysis. The device has been out of production for at least forty years. It's actually considered an illegal firework, nearly the explosive equivalent of an 'M80,' an extra powerful firecracker that's now banned throughout the U.S." He added, "An obsolete ignition noisemaker is not the sort of gizmo a high school kid would have at his or her fingertips."

"Unless his or her parents had one tucked away in their attic."

"Perhaps. Although I don't see installing a noisemaker as the sort of prank that high school kids would pull—particularly hip kids who are trying to be clever rather than vindictive."

"Hmm. I didn't find the Bug on my porch all that clever."

Rafe wondered if she intended to challenge every comment he made. *At least she's paying close attention.*

"Let me give you another interesting piece of information," he said. "We also learned from the NCSBI that the notes the Phantom Avenger left at the original series of pranks were printed using an ink-jet printer. However, the note that accompanied the stink bomb and the note you found in Lily Kirk's car were printed on a laser printer."

"What are you suggesting?" Emma asked.

Rafe overpowered the urge to say, *Isn't it obvious?*

"I think there are two different Phantom Avengers—one funny, the other destructive."

"But why would the Contemporaries do that? A pair of Avengers doesn't serve any purpose."

Rafe shrugged. "That's the part I haven't figured out yet." He began to eat his SOG-gy Burger.

"Speaking of figuring things out—do you know why the noisemaker didn't explode when Lily started the Taurus?"

"We do, thanks again to the NCSBI." Rafe paused to swallow a mouthful of burger. "Your classic ignition noisemaker is designed to be wired to the exposed electric terminals on a car's starter motor. Back in the fifties and sixties, the terminals were out in the open, very easy to reach.

"When the driver turns the key, the starter motor cranks, the noisemaker goes *bang,* and the driver panics. Everyone watching has a big laugh.

"But whoever installed the noisemaker in Lily's car attached its wires to the horn circuit on the Taurus. The device exploded the first time she blew the horn." He let himself frown. "That seems an uncertain way of playing a prank on her. Lily might not have tooted her horn for months."

Rafe watched Emma's face go pale. "Animals," she murmured.

"Animals?"

"Lily told me that she often used her horn to warn deer and raccoons that she was barreling down the road."

He leaned forward, all the while grappling with the frisson of excitement that made him want to shout follow-up questions. Emma McCall had just provided genuinely useful information—possibly the scrap of evidence that proved the existence of a second Phantom Avenger? How much more information did she have?

Don't push too hard. Slow and steady keeps witnesses ready.

"We know," he said calmly, "that Lily was coming back from Elizabeth City. She'd bought a powerful magnifying glass in a hobby shop on West Ehringhaus Street. We found the lens in her purse. Do you think she was in a hurry to get back to Glory?"

"A big hurry," Emma said. "I told you why the other day. Lily planned to attend the meeting of Sara Knoll's writer's club at my B and B."

Rafe nodded. "Lily died on a relatively straight stretch of Route 34A my daughter calls 'the forest primeval.' It's a good place to accelerate if you need to make up time. In fact, it's the first real opportunity to speed this side of Elizabeth City. It's also a notorious deer crossing."

"A perfect place for Lily to blow the horn to alert local wildlife."

Rafe inclined back in his chair. "Do you think that

many other people knew about Lily's horn-blowing habits?"

"Not many. Lots of folks knew that Lily liked to drive without wearing her seat belt, but she considered fast driving 'her little secret.' She shared that failing with only with a few friends. At least, that's what she told me."

Rafe found it difficult not to stand up and cheer.

"Well, let's assume that you're a favored friend of Lily who has ridden in her car before. If you know that she's returning from Elizabeth City, you might expect her to toot her horn when she reaches 'the forest primeval.' And, because you also know that Lily skimps on car maintenance, you might guess that an ignition noisemaker would have enough explosive *oomph* to pop open her car's hood."

"If the Phantom Avenger knew all that when he planted the noisemaker—" Emma's brow furrowed "—doesn't that make it a more serious crime than involuntary manslaughter?"

"You're absolutely right. I'd call it intentional murder." Rafe leaned toward Emma once more. "I'm now positive there are two Phantom Avengers. The first—played by a group of high school students—is a prankster. The second—identity unknown—is a cold-blooded killer."

Emma coughed. She reached for her cappuccino and drank deeply. She put down the mug and said, "That's awful! I hate to sound mercenary, but every cent I have is invested in The Scottish Captain. If the media finds out that an ersatz Phantom Avenger is killing people, we'll see a news blitz that will devastate Glory's tourist industry—and probably put me out of business."

Rafe took a moment to consider Emma's reaction.

*She has her own good reasons for wanting an incon-
spicuous investigation.*

"Funny you should say that," he said. "I don't want
the word to leak out, either. Most people won't believe
there are two Phantom Avengers. They'll jump to the
conclusion that the Contemporaries killed Lily because
she was the leader of the Traditionalists."

Emma lowered her voice. "Can a policeman keep an
intentional murder secret?"

"I'm not keeping any crime secret. With your help,
I evaluated the limited evidence we have gathered so far
and came up with a highly speculative theory. I'd be
foolish to go public with my conclusions without solid
evidence, including proof of the identity of the second
Phantom Avenger."

She smiled at him. "That line of reasoning will
probably work for a few days," she said. "But we can't
take too long to find the killer Avenger. The media is
becoming inquisitive."

"We?"

"Lily Kirk told me she was in danger. I should have
made her talk to the police, but I didn't. I can't turn back
the clock and undo what happened, but I can make
certain that her death isn't ignored. Let me help, or *I'll*
talk to the reporters."

Rafe read the utter determination in Emma's eyes
and decided not to argue. After all, there wasn't much
downside if he kept her informed. He had intended to
do that much, anyway.

*You'll make the important decisions. She's nothing
but a bystander.*

TEN

Emma set the pile of newspapers to her left on the sofa in the front parlor and placed the steaming mug of flavored coffee on the lamp table to her right. She made herself comfortable on the sofa and began to read.

Emma loved Sunday afternoons at The Scottish Captain. She thought of them as battery chargers—precious periods of solitude to read the Sunday papers, watch a movie, or curl up with a novel. She wasn't quite sure why, but guests who'd spent the weekend at the Captain invariably left after breakfast on Sunday morning and new arrivals never seemed to arrive before Sunday evening. More often than not, she could count on seven or eight peaceful hours with few responsibilities.

Emma felt a bit edgier than usual on this Sunday afternoon, though, because there was a chance—slim but real—that the regional newspapers had joined the Greenville TV station's "campaign" against hooliganism in Glory.

She scoured the pages of the *Raleigh News and Observer*. No mention of Glory or the Phantom Avenger, or—most worrisome of all to Emma—the fact that Simon Rogers had spent three nights at The Scottish Captain. She moved on to the *Daily Reflector* from Greenville. Also nothing. She even checked the *New York Times.* Ditto.

Emma murmured, "No news is great news," and began to flip through the *Times*'s magazine section.

She needed a moment to interpret the bell-like sound that she heard in the distance. It seemed strident and insistent, not at all akin to the calming *bong* of a church bell. Emma suddenly realized that she had fallen asleep while reading the newspaper, that the telephone was ringing in her office and that the wall was shut.

Whoever designed the residence building that became the Captain had made provision for a small office—a windowless room that measured about seven by seven—adjacent to the front parlor on the first floor. The really odd thing about the office was its thick sliding "pocket door" that had been papered in the same pattern as the parlor. When open, the extrawide door disappeared into the parlor's wall. When shut, the door's wallpapered surface seemed an integral part of the wall. The door might have been difficult to locate, except for the large brass door handle near the right edge.

She slid off the sofa, moved clumsily to the pocket door and pushed the handle to the left. She reached the phone on her desk seconds after the answering machine had switched on: *You've dialed The Scottish Captain. This is Emma McCall. I'm unavailable right now, but if you'll leave a message…*

She yanked the receiver out of its cradle. "Hi. This is Emma McCall."

"And this is Rafe Neilson. You sound like I woke you."

"You did, but I shouldn't have been sleeping."

"How about a tall mug of coffee to wake you up?"

"A good idea. I think I have some in the kitchen…"

"I mean at *my* place. I've been studying our background file on Lily Kirk. I think you might want to see it."

Emma considered the invitation. "I suppose we can get together," she said, hesitantly, still thinking about the new mystery novel she had intended to start.

"The file is scattered across my dining room table," Rafe said quickly.

Emma realized that he had misread her indecision. Before she could clear up the confusion, he continued, "You coming here is easier than me going there. We'll even have a…*um*…chaperone, my daughter, Kate." He added, "I don't think you two have ever met."

Emma heard a definite quiver of discomfort in his voice. The idea that Rafe Nielson, ace police investigator, found it both necessary—and awkward—to speak the word "chaperone" amused her.

Decide what you want to do. The ball's in your court.

"What time did you have in mind?" she said.

"How about now?"

Emma glanced at her desk clock. Two-fifteen. With luck, she would still have some time to delve into murder and mayhem in jolly old England.

"Now works for me."

"Good. I'll zip over in my 'Vette and pick you up."

He hung up before Emma could decline the offer of a ride. A short walk would have cleared her still-muzzy brain.

Ugh! He'll be here in less than a minute.

Emma couldn't help smiling when she climbed out of the Corvette. She had often walked down Front Street and admired the pretty little Victorian bungalow covered with blue clapboard and miles of gingerbread trimming. It seemed hard to believe that a policeman owned it.

"What's so funny?" Rafe asked.

"Every time I see this house, I think what a fabulous B and B it would make if it was only twice its size. Honeymooners would fight to spend a few nights in such lovely surroundings. And your view of Albemarle Sound is spectacular."

"You sound just like my daughter. One look and she knew where she wanted to live. I guess fancy woodwork is a woman thing."

"Absolutely," Emma said. She felt a burst of admiration for Rafe as he unlocked the front door. This was clearly not a house that a man would choose for himself. What were the chances that his daughter appreciated the sacrifice he had made for her? *Not very high.*

Emma followed Rafe through a tiny foyer, past a living room that seemed overfilled with upholstered furniture and into a small dining room that could seat eight at most. There were brown wooden chair rails on the walls, with beige wood paneling below and yellow patterned wallpaper above. The draperies were also yellow; the sheers inside a muted ivory. The beige-and-brown oriental rug atop the parquet flooring gave the room an elegant feel.

Rafe guided Emma to the far side of a cherrywood pedestal dining table that had become a makeshift desk. She sat down in front of three piles of photographs— the left pile of Lily Kirk's car, the center of Lily herself, the right of what must be Lily's home.

"How would you like your coffee?" he asked.

"Cream and a little sugar. An unexpected feeling of

melancholy welled up inside her as she remembered the many times that Charlie made coffee for her when they were first married. The feeling intensified as she realized that this was the first time a man had offered her home-brewed coffee since the divorce.

"Coffee coming right up!" Rafe said. He pushed through a pair of swinging café doors into a kitchen that seemed to echo the brown-beige-yellow color scheme of the dining room.

Would he also offer her a tour of the house? she wondered. Probably not. Men rarely thought about showing off their homes. Pity! She might never get another chance.

She looked around the dining room again and concluded that Kate must have exercised considerable influence when the house was furnished. The only masculine item in sight was an oil painting of an early nineteenth century warship—perhaps an American frigate—splashing through a rough sea.

Rafe returned gripping a coffee mug in his right hand and Kate Neilson's arm in his left.

"Emma," he said, "meet my daughter, Kate." His voice became noticeably firmer. "Kate, this is Miss McCall. She owns The Scottish Captain."

Emma recognized Kate straight away, despite the hostile expression chiseled into her pretty face. Emma had seen her in Glory on several occasions and in church from time to time but hadn't known her name.

Emma held out her hand. Kate took it as if she was picking up a putrid dishrag. "Good day, Miss McCall." Her icy tone signaled her wish that Emma leave *her* house immediately.

"Kate is fifteen," Rafe said.

"Great, Dad, thanks for sharing."

Emma glanced at Rafe. His pained but clueless expression, embellished with a tinge of embarrassment, was almost funny.

Well, let's find out why Kate is being aggressively unfriendly.

"Your dad told me that you are a dyed-in-the-wool Contemporary at church," Emma said. "You're even committed enough to be part of the leadership team."

"That's true." Kate smiled slyly. "He told me that you're a Nothing."

Touché!

Emma bit her tongue. She didn't want to laugh in Kate's face or exchange insults with a fifteen-year-old. However, a snappy comeback seemed in order.

Emma imitated Kate's moue. "I'll bet he said that before he got to know me as well as he does now."

Double touché!

Kate's eye's widened, her face became a mask. "Uh, I have to finish an essay now." She made an exaggerated U-turn around Rafe and left the dining room.

When Kate was out of earshot, he said, "My apologies. Kate is a well-mannered kid, but I've been warned to expect this kind of reaction from her. She misses her mother a lot. I suppose that's why she misinterpreted your presence here today."

He sat down opposite Emma and stared at the wall over her head. "You're the first single woman to visit this house since we moved to Glory. Kate must be wary of you intruding on the life we're building together. She's probably also protecting her mother's memory."

Emma sipped her coffee and dredged up a surge of sympathy for motherless Kate Neilson. She tried to remember what she'd been like at age fifteen. Independent. Arrogant. Determined to do things her way. Sometimes brash, sometimes timid. Confident one moment, uncertain the next. Rafe clearly was trying to be a good parent, but some of his comments about Kate suggested that he didn't fully understand his daughter's mind.

No surprise. When I was a teenager, there were lots of things about me that my father never understood.

"To the contrary, Rafe," Emma said, "Kate is trying to protect you."

"Me?"

"Oh, yes. Our merry banter was about your reaction to me."

"Are you sure?"

"Completely. I've been weighed in the balance and found wanting. Kate doesn't consider me good enough for you."

"But…but…how can that be?" Rafe's gaze darted back and forth like a trapped animal searching desperately for a way out. "You haven't been here before, we haven't…"

"Gone out on a date?"

"Exactly!"

"Rafe, you're forgetting that Kate is both intelligent and resourceful. Glory is a small town. I'll wager that she's cataloged the entire population of single women. She probably has several candidates in mind for the role of wife and stepmother. I didn't make her short list."

"Girls actually do that?"

"I wouldn't be surprised if she got her friends to help with the project."

"But…but…"

"You're beginning to sound like an outboard motor."

"That's because my head is spinning." He held up his hand. "Who started this conversation about me?"

"You did, but I'm perfectly willing to switch topics." She held up her mug in a toast. "You make a great cup of coffee."

Rafe answered the toast with a crisp salute. "Thank you for noticing." He beamed at her. "I started out as one of those husbands who felt lost around a kitchen. I could boil water, cook eggs, toast bread and open a can of soup and that was about it. When Kim was killed, I had to learn how to cook real meals. Kate knew enough to be my tutor. Making good coffee was an integral part of my training."

Emma sipped from her mug and marveled at his resiliency. Rafe didn't seem bitter. He had found the strength to deal with his enormous pain and had also managed to raise a headstrong daughter by himself.

"Moving right along…" Rafe inhaled deeply, reached for a manila file folder, and said, "How good a friend of Lily's, were you?"

"I hardly knew Lily. She considered me an acquaintance—nothing more. In fact, she addressed me as 'Mrs. McCall' on the night before she died."

"And yet, she sought you out to share her fears and concerns. How do you explain that?"

"Lily saw us talking at choir practice that night. We must have looked like…"

"An *item?*"

"There's a phrase I haven't heard in years, but yes, I think she assumed we had some sort of relationship. In any case, she wanted my advice on whether she should talk to you. I told you why at the accident scene. Lily was afraid you'd laugh at her."

Rafe opened the folder and slid a thin document

across the table. "Two of my officers attended the funeral yesterday. They interviewed several of the mourners before and after the service and expanded the biographical sketch that the library had on file. I added a few notes about Lily that I made when I interviewed Nina McEwen." He leaned back in his chair. "It's only three pages long. Lily led a quiet, mostly private life."

Emma began reading the sketch and soon found herself caught up in the bittersweet tale of a girl from Glory who moved to New York City with dreams of becoming a Broadway star.

She sighed softly. The terse summary of Lily's life made it almost seem that she didn't have one. But who was Emma McCall to make statements like that? Half the folks in Glory probably thought the very same thing about her. Kate Neilson, for one.

"I see that Lily never married," she said.

"Nope. Moreover, when Lily returned to Glory, she became a near recluse. She didn't have many friends."

"That's sad…" Emma abruptly stopped pushing the document back toward Rafe. "And strange! Lily Kirk mysteriously changed from a musical comedy performer in New York City to a loner in Glory. "What could trigger such a radical metamorphosis?"

"Now you're thinking like a detective." Rafe placed a single sheet of paper in front of Emma. She peered at it. It was a barely readable fax of an old document that had been prepared with a typewriter.

"Is this what I think it is?" Emma asked.

"Yep. Lily Kirk had a criminal record. She served ten months in a Manhattan lockup for theft."

"My goodness." She quickly added, "What did Lily steal?"

"She stole two theatrical props in use at the Bleecker Street Playhouse, where she'd taken a backstage job during the summer of 1967. Specifically, Lily copped a pair of eighteenth-century dueling pistols that had been borrowed from the New York City Museum to dress up a Russian costume drama.

"The two guns were considered genuine antiquities and were worth a bundle. She subsequently sold one to an antique shop in Philadelphia. She told the owner that it been left to her by a wealthy relative. She hid the second pistol, and the money she received from the first, inside a hollowed-out upholstered footrest in her apartment."

"*Our* Lily Kirk did all that?"

"Never, *ever* judge a book by its cover. That's the first rule of detective work."

"So it was going to prison that transformed her?"

Rafe nodded. "The way I figure it, she kept her sins a secret when she returned to Glory, took an underpaid job as the town librarian and lived like a semihermit so that no one would pry into her past."

"Do we have to reveal Lily's secret? It would be a shame to tell her few friends in town that she spent time behind bars."

"I agree with you." He slipped the sheet of paper back into the file folder. "If there's no pressing reason to make her record public, I won't."

"Fair enough," Emma said. "What's next?"

"That depends on what you want to see." He gestured, without his earlier animation, Emma thought, toward the papers on the table. "Name your pleasure— police reports, photographs, eyewitness statements? I agreed to keep you informed and everything is here."

"But…?"

He softened his shrug with a cautious smile. "But none of them will tell you anything new. You already know everything we do."

She stared at the papers on the table and asked herself which part of Rafe's comment had elicited the hazy twinges of disappointment she felt.

"Yes, well, then I'd best return to the mystery novel that's waiting for me on my coffee table."

One of these days, I'll ask Rafe for a nickel tour of this house. I'll bet he'll say yes.

"That sounds…nice," he said. "I'll drive you home."

"No need. It's a pretty day for a short walk."

"Makes sense to me—a walk before reading."

Emma tried to sort out the curious expression that had mysteriously appeared on Rafe's face—a peculiar mixture of unhappy and bewildered. She realized that she also felt vaguely upset, almost wishing that she had a reason to stay. Perhaps she was beginning to enjoy police work?

What else could it be?

"Anything new happen that I should know about?"

Rafe looked up at Chief Porter and nodded. "I met with Emma McCall on Saturday and again yesterday afternoon."

"She still mad at us?"

"Nope. We are getting along splendidly."

"Good. I'd rather have her inside the tent throwing rocks at people outside than the other way around."

Rafe grunted in agreement. He'd been the target of Emma's thrown rocks, and her aim improved as she became upset. He said, "Believe it or not, I think she's going to be of significant help to us."

"You've got to be kidding!" The Chief dropped into a visitor's chair and peered intently at Rafe.

The Chief's astonished reaction didn't surprise Rafe. On the way to work this Monday morning, he'd mused about how Emma's astute judgment had caught him off guard.

"She's a good thinker," Rafe said, "and she has several solid insights into Lily Kirk's behavior. It seems that Lily and Emma had a woman's heart-to-heart conversation the evening before Lily was murdered."

Rafe groaned inwardly. He hadn't meant to use the *M* word.

"What murder?" the Chief blurted. "When I left on Friday we were talking about the crime of involuntary manslaughter—at the very worst."

"Lily Kirk was murdered by a cold-blooded killer—a copycat Phantom Avenger—who tried to make it look like she was the victim of a failed practical joke."

"Are you sure?"

"Yes, but I'm not going to tell you anything more. That way you won't have to lie if you get a call from a reporter."

"What do I say should a gentleman of the press call?"

"Explain that we're investigating a fatal automobile accident. Then pass him to me."

"And Emma McCall is okay with keeping the lid on?"

"Yep. She thinks she's part of my team."

"Sir?" a woman's voice said.

Rafe looked up and saw Angie Ringgold approaching his desk. "Yes, Angie?"

"A call just came in that you definitely want to know about. There's been a break-in at Lily Kirk's town house."

"Who reported it?"

"The neighbor in the adjacent unit. She was walking her dog behind the complex and noticed an open back door on the Kirk town house. She took a closer look and saw that the door had been pried open and the interior torn apart. She insists that the door was closed last night."

"Get on over there, Angie. Secure the property, but be careful. Make sure that the perp isn't still browsing around inside. I'll be there in a few minutes."

Rafe turned to Chief Porter. "Do you mind if I bring Emma McCall?"

The Chief grinned. "It's your decision, but that's absolutely the last question I'd ever expect you to ask. Is something else going on that I should know about?"

"Very funny! The answer is a big, emphatic *NO*."

Rafe started the Corvette then dialed The Scottish Captain on his cell phone. Emma answered on the second ring. He interrupted her hello.

"Someone ransacked Lily Kirk's town house. I'm on my way to inspect the scene. Do you want to come along?"

The line went quiet for several seconds. "Who'll complain if I leave the dirty breakfast dishes for later?" Emma said. "I own the place."

"Good thinking. I'll pick you up in forty-five seconds."

Lily's town house was in the northwest corner of Glory on Queen Street. A clever builder had squeezed seven narrow three-story homes into the short block between Albemarle and Oliver Streets. Rafe parked the 'Vette behind Angie Ringgold's police cruiser.

The morning was chilly. Rafe zipped up his duty jacket; he watched Emma pull her coat tighter. He guided her around the cluster of town houses to a narrow grassy area that ran behind all seven homes.

"Do you think the same person planted the noise-maker and broke in to her home?" Emma asked.

"You're jumping three squares ahead, but I had the same thought."

He waved at Angie, who was standing near the back door of the middle town house.

"What did you find?" he said.

"The place has been thoroughly trashed. The perp must have worked all night."

Rafe took the lead. The back door opened into a small laundry and mudroom. Both washing machine and dryer had been pulled away from the wall.

The laundry room connected to a paneled family room. The draperies were tightly drawn. Rafe located a light switch.

"Wow," Emma said, as she surveyed the overturned furniture, the ripped-open sofa, the snowstorm of papers distributed around the room. "Whoever did this is a maniac."

"Maybe not. It looks to me like the perp was searching for something specific. Lily must have done a good job of hiding it because some of the damage appears to have been done for spite." He pointed toward a smashed wall mirror and a menagerie of broken ceramic animals in a fallen display case.

Rafe handed Emma a pair of latex gloves. "Put them on before you touch anything—" he smiled at her "—if you decide to ignore my order not to touch anything."

"Okay, okay. I won't compromise any potential evidence."

"Let's head upstairs. The kitchen and living room are on the next level."

The living room, Rafe discovered, was also in tatters, but surprisingly little had been destroyed in the kitchen.

Lily's pots and pans were still in their cupboards, her crockery still on the shelves.

"Why spare the kitchen?" he murmured.

Emma heard him and said, "Because tossing pots around and smashing dinner plates make lots of noise. This was done late at night, remember?"

"Why didn't I think of that?" He pointed to the ceiling. "One flight to go. The bedrooms are on the second level."

Rafe wished he had brought a nuisance dust mask when he saw the master bedroom. The innards of Lily's queen-size mattress lay in clumps across the floor, partially covering the clothing and shoes that had been pulled from her closet.

"Look at this," Emma said. "The perp left Emma's jewelry drawer alone."

Rafe turned around. Emma was standing in front of a chest of drawers placed against the wall opposite Lily's bed. All but one of the drawers had been taken out, their contents emptied in a large pile. The one survivor was the chest's shallow, topmost drawer.

"How do you know that's where Lily kept her jewelry?"

"Duh!" Emma made a face. "*Every* woman who owns a chest of drawers keeps her jewelry in that drawer."

He opened the drawer. Jewelry.

"I learn something new every day." He slid the drawer shut. "Now we have more evidence that burglary wasn't the motive. Onward to the second bedroom."

"Yikes," Emma said when she pushed open the door. "What's all this stuff?"

Rafe righted a folding table that lay upside down on the floor. Scattered around it were pieces of leather, scraps of different fabrics, sheets of decorative papers, several oddly shaped knives, a handful of plastic implements that resembled medical tongue depressors and two glass jars. He retrieved one of the jars and read its label. Bookbinders' Glue. A thick adhesive that is transparent when dry. Holds to most materials and will not curl paper.

Across the small room, four corrugated cardboard boxes—once full of old books that now lay piled on the floor—had been upended. An old wooden chair lay atop the mound of books.

"This must be Lily's workshop," he said. "She kept her hand in by repairing damaged books from the church library."

Rafe heard a sniffle behind him.

"What's wrong?" he said to Emma.

"Don't look at me. I'm crying."

"Ah." He turned away, wondering if he should give in to the unexpected urge he felt to comfort her.

"The skunk that did this obliterated everything Lily had," Emma said, "even her volunteer work for the church."

"We'll catch him, Emma. That's a promise."

"I have a promise in return. You had better find the person responsible, *or I will.*"

ELEVEN

Emma sat completely still.

Her strategy was simple. If she remained motionless, the overbearing agent from the North Caroline State Bureau of Investigation might ignore her. It seemed to be working. He was standing in front of the whiteboard and hadn't looked her way for at least two minutes, even though his body language continued to proclaim his annoyance that she, a mere civilian, had been admitted to an official police meeting. Moreover, the agent in question had decided to take his displeasure out on Rafe Neilson.

"I've thought about it, Rafe, and I dispute most of what you've said. I read your memos and studied the evidence—I don't see a grain of support for your theory that a copycat Phantom Avenger is responsible."

"Then let me take you through my argument again," Rafe said.

"No. I'll show you why your argument fails. You've put together three items of wishful thinking that fly in the face of solid facts. Lily Kirk died as a result of a stupid prank pulled by a bunch of high school kids. That's what the evidence you've gathered says. There's only one question left—what will the Glory police do about it?"

Emma glanced at Rafe; he looked thoroughly angry, about to explode. She shut her eyes and wished he hadn't invited her to this silly meeting.

Rafe had called after lunch. "I've scheduled a routine status briefing at four-thirty this afternoon to discuss Lily's death," he said. "You've been a great help to my investigation, so I thought—actually, I wondered—do you want to come and listen? You might find it interesting, unless of course you're too busy taking care of guests."

"I'll be there," she had replied. "I have only one guest tonight and no other bookings until Sunday."

"Really?"

The surprise in his voice prompted her to add, "The middle two weeks in November are unpredictable. Some years, Glory is chock-full of snowbirds driving south. Other years—like this one—we're not very busy."

Emma didn't explain that she had planned to use the free time to redecorate one of her guest rooms but that concentrating on routine chores had become all but impossible because her thoughts kept returning to Lily Kirk. At least Hancock Jeffers would make good use of the Captain's downtime. He had assembled a long list of maintenance chores.

Emma arrived at the police station at four twenty-five and found Rafe with a cheerful grin on his face waiting for her in the lobby.

"I'm glad you could make it," he said.

"I've never been to a 'routine status briefing' before."

"You'll absolutely, positively love it…unless you fall asleep, like the Chief usually does."

Emma followed Rafe to a small, windowless conference room at the rear of the building. Three of its walls were painted institutional lime green; the fourth was covered with whiteboard tiles to create a floor-to-ceiling writing surface. A square conference table took up most of the room's floor space. It had a transparent plastic top with a large-scale map of Glory laminated beneath the surface. The only other furniture in the room was a collection of eight dissimilar chairs—some wood, some metal, some with upholstered seats and some without.

Chief Porter acknowledged Emma with a tip of his head. He gestured toward the striking man sitting to his right and spoke an introduction that Emma didn't fully catch: "Emma, this is Ty—something—of the NCSBI." The man had piercing black eyes, a rosy complexion and a completely shaven head. He was bigger than either the Chief or Rafe and seemed to overflow his chair. Before she could ask the Chief to repeat his name, Rafe began talking.

"Thank you all for coming. I'm going to tape our meeting so we'll have a transcript of the proceedings." He pushed the record button on a cassette recorder that sat in the center of the square table.

"This is a status briefing to review the progress of our investigation of the death of Lily Kirk, age sixty-four, a resident of Glory, North Carolina, who was killed on Thursday, 9 November, at approximately 4:15 p.m. in an apparent automobile accident at Mile Marker 16.2 on State Route 34A. Today's date is Monday, 13 November. It's 4:32 p.m. Present are Chief Gary Porter, Glory Police Department...Deputy Chief Rafe Neilson, Glory Police Department...Special Agent Tyrone Keefe, North Carolina State Bureau of Investigation...and Ms. Emma McCall."

Emma had brought a small notebook with her. She jotted down *Tyrone Keefe—NCSBI*.

Rafe continued. "I'll begin by summarizing our findings to date. The victim apparently lost control of her 1989 Ford Taurus sedan when a so-called ignition noise-maker—a powerful, explosive firework—detonated and caused the hood to rise to the open position, blocking her view of the road ahead. The device had been wired to the vehicle's horn in such a way that sounding the horn would cause the device to explode. A note printed on a five-inch-by-seven-inch white file card, discovered taped to the inside of the vehicle's hood, claimed that the device had been placed by the 'Phantom Avenger.'

"We recovered debris left after the explosion of the noisemaker and sent it to the NCSBI Crime Laboratory in Raleigh, North Carolina, along with the file card. Their laboratory technicians did not find any finger-prints or any other latent evidence that might identify the person or persons responsible."

"Point of order, Rafe," Agent Keefe said.

"Yes, Ty?"

"Is Ms. McCall a civilian?" He said "civilian" with a sneering hiss.

Rafe nodded cautiously. "Yes."

"I'm not thrilled discussing NCSBI work in the presence of a civilian."

"I can vouch for her discretion."

"Can you now?" Keefe peered at Emma suspiciously for a moment then mumbled something unintelligible.

Emma jotted S-I-T next to Ty's name and under-lined the letters. Tyrone Keefe struck her as a perfect example of a "self-important twit." Haughtiness and pretentiousness seemed to ooze from every pore.

Rafe went on. "Subsequent examination of the vehicle's hood latch release, wiring harness and engine compartment surfaces surrounding the horn failed to find fingerprints or other latent evidence.

"Given the victim's habit of blowing her horn while speeding though heavily treed areas, we've concluded that the ignition noisemaker was probably installed while Ms. Kirk was shopping in Elizabeth City. Based on her destination in Elizabeth City, she likely parked her car on Westover Street, just north of West Ehringhause Street.

"We've also concluded that the person or persons responsible for Ms. Kirk's death are not the parties who perpetrated a series of practical jokes in Glory, also under the rubric of 'Phantom Avenger.'"

Emma flinched when Ty Keefe pounded the table with his closed fist. "I disagree." He stood up, moved to the whiteboard wall, uncapped a black marker pen and made his speech about opposing everything Rafe said. He then began talking toward the wall as he scribbled words on the whiteboard.

1. No proof of Elizabeth City!

"You have five reasons for assuming there's a second, homicidal Phantom Avenger on the loose. First, you argue that the noisemaker was installed in Elizabeth City. Frankly, we don't know when it was installed. All we can say is that it exploded when the victim blew the horn. Now, you say that high school students wouldn't be clever enough to attach the device to the horn wiring. Why not? The horn terminals are easy to reach in a hurry, whereas the starter motor is half-hidden under the engine. I'll also guess that half the town knew that Lily Kirk was a speeder who liked to toot the horn. That's not the kind of behavior that stays secret in a small town."

2.The kids didn't care what the noisemaker would do!

"Second, you say that perpetrator believed that the noisemaker would pop the hood of the old Taurus. Why? It's much more plausible that your students assumed the device would go *bang,* and that would be the end of it. I don't believe they set out to murder Lily Kirk. It was everyone's dumb luck that a foolish prank turned fatal. It's too bad, but the kids will have to answer for what they did."

3.We'll figure out where the kids got the exploder.

"Third, you believe that high school students would have difficulty acquiring an ignition noisemaker because the device hasn't been produced in nearly forty years. We know that at least one of the gizmos survived intact in Glory. The easiest explanation is that the students found a carton of the things in someone's basement. You've got to press the kids harder, find out who provided the device."

4.There are hundreds of laser printers in Glory!

"Fourth, you think it's important that the Phantom Avenger notes were printed on two different printers. I have both an ink-jet and a laser in my office at home. I'm sure that both varieties are available in your high school. The mere fact that the Avenger used two methods of printing doesn't prove a thing."

5. Where's the connection between the prank and the robbery?

"Fifth, you argue there's a connection between Lily Kirk's death and the break-in at her home. Well, the most credible connection is that you have an opportunist in Glory who decided to see what might be up for grabs in her town house now that the woman is dead. There's absolutely no evidence that the same person planted the noisemaker and jimmied the back door open."

Ty capped the marker pen and turned around. "Rafe, you're a smart cop, so stop beating a dead horse. It's been more than forty-eight hours since the killing. I know what that means and so do you. There's a zero chance that you'll find more evidence or new witnesses. It won't happen. You have all the evidence you're going to have. There won't be anything new. And the evidence on hand points to a single, teenage perpetrator."

Emma glanced again at Rafe and saw a change in his body language. He seemed more disheartened than angry. The Chief appeared equally dispirited. He had rocked his chair backward on its two rear legs and was staring at the whiteboard, as if he'd decided not to look at Rafe or Ty. Mercifully, everyone seemed to be ignoring her presence.

She looked back at Rafe. *What's happening here is not fair to him.* Almost without thinking about it, Emma stood up. "Mr. Keefe, it's my turn to disagree with you," she said to the special agent. He gawked at her as if she had slapped his face. The Chief let the front legs of his chair slam forward to the floor.

Rafe murmured a soft, "Emma, what are you doing?"

"I beg your pardon?" Ty said, making each syllable sound like a threat.

"You should beg all our pardons." Emma tried to match the tone of her voice to his. "Your summary of the facts conveniently ignores an essential piece of evidence."

"And what evidence would that be?"

"On the day before Lily Kirk died, the driver of a pickup truck tried to run her off the road. When that didn't work, the killer invented Plan B. He installed the noisemaker in Lily's car and tried to blame the Phantom Avenger. Think about it—the original Phantom Avenger was a jokester, his objective was to do funny things to call attention to the dispute. The original pranks had panache. There's nothing funny or stylish about planting a stink bomb or installing an explosive device that frightens someone."

Emma decided to remain standing. She anticipated a counter barrage from Tyrone Keefe. Sitting down would give him a psychological advantage.

"You're perfectly right, Ms. McCall," he said, "I did ignore the speculation that the victim was threatened by a pickup truck. Notice that I said 'speculation,' not evidence. All we have to substantiate the event is your report that Ms. Kirk made a statement to you. I don't like hearsay testimony. I don't consider it real evidence."

"You seem to imply that I'm an unreliable witness."

"Those are your words, not mine, but I remain unimpressed by your claims of road violence or your arguments about the relative humor of different pranks. The book of jokes circulated at the high school—each of the pranks was perpetrated by a different student. We would expect some pranks to be joyful and others to be mean-spirited." An angry scowl settled on his face. "Now, if you don't mind, please sit down, shut up and leave police work to professionals who know what they are doing. Better yet, go home and watch a detective drama on TV. You can figure out *whodunit* without doing damage to real police work."

"Whoa!" Rafe shouted as he rose from his chair. "There's no need for that sort of discourtesy, Ty. The Glory Police Department asked Ms. McCall to participate in the investigation. This is *our* headquarters building."

"Have it your way." Ty lobbed the marker pen to the center of the conference table. It rolled along the surface and tumbled to the floor near the Chief's chair. "You clearly have an agenda, Rafe, and whatever you're trying to accomplish is interfering with your common sense. I hope you know what you're doing."

Emma stepped aside to let the big man stride to the door of the conference room. "See you around, Chief," he said over his shoulder. Emma expected him to slam the door, but he swung it shut behind him with only a slight thud.

"Well," Chief Porter said, "that was an interesting end to a fascinating meeting. I'm glad we didn't have a shoot-out."

"It was my fault," Emma said, "I shouldn't have challenged him."

"He's not mad at you," Rafe said. "He's mad at me."

"You got that right," the Chief said. "He may also have given us a sound piece of advice. We may have to move ahead with the evidence we have." He waved his hand toward Rafe in a gesture of dismissal. "Go home. Forget about the case until tomorrow." He peered up at Emma. "I suggest that you do the same, Ms. McCall."

Emma watched Rafe nod unhappily and make for the door. She followed him through the building and into the parking lot. He stopped in front of his Corvette.

"I'll drive you home," he said.

"Thanks, but I can use a walk. I want to clear Tyrone Keefe from my head."

"That's a great idea. Let's do it together over dinner. Come with me to The Glorious Table. My treat."

"You're asking me out?" She realized too late that her voice had climbed an octave.

Why should a gracious invitation cause such a fluster?

Rafe seem mystified for a moment, but then he began to smile. "If you put it that way, Emma, I suppose I am. What do you say?"

"Oh…" Emma rapidly regained her composure. "Well, I guess I'd like to."

Is that the best you can do? Now you're babbling.

Rafe's smile deepened. He didn't seem to mind her childish reaction to his invitation.

"I'll drop you at home, and then pick you up—" he glanced at his watch "—at five-thirty."

She did a mental calculation. *Twenty minutes isn't enough time to choose a new outfit and freshen my makeup.*

"Make it six," she said. Her mouth began to feel dry.

What on earth is going on? Why am I in such a panic? Why am I so wound up about going to dinner?

Rafe paused in front of The Scottish Captain feeling oddly bemused. He couldn't remember actually deciding to ask Emma McCall to have dinner with him. His invitation seemed to have sprung from his throat all by itself. He'd been as astonished to speak his words as she had been to hear them.

Well, maybe not. Emma's greater astonishment had made her forget to insist that they go dutch treat.

Rafe checked his watch. Two minutes to six. *Better not rush her.* That was a simple rule. He leaned against a lamppost on Broad Street and contemplated the Captain. The front of the building was brightly lit by four large floodlights buried in the lawn. The sun had set about a half hour earlier, so the clear sky above the building was dark blue rather than black. The scene would make an ideal photo, Rafe thought, for Glory's tourist brochure.

Time to go. Don't keep her waiting.

Rafe climbed the steps to the front porch, pushed the doorbell and heard the chime ring inside. The door swung open almost immediately. Emma stood there smiling at him, stunning in a soft wool dress that showcased her figure.

Say something flattering—now!

"You look lovely."

"Why thank you, Rafe. You're pretty nifty, yourself. I like Harris tweed jackets."

He offered Emma his arm. She took it without protest. He set an easy pace and guided her north along Broad Street. A couple walking south gazed curiously at Rafe, then at Emma, and then back at Rafe.

"I think we've been *spotted*," Emma said. "They seem to know us."

"They're new members of the church," he replied. "Bob and Phyllis *something.*"

"By tomorrow, Glory will know we went walking arm in arm."

"The joys of a small town."

"That reminds me. What did you tell Kate?"

"I told her that I invited you to dinner."

"And she said…"

Rafe switched to a falsetto voice. "Dad, you're old enough to make your own decisions."

"And you said…"

"You aren't. Finish all your homework before you watch TV."

Emma laughed just as a small brown-and-white Jack Russell terrier darted out onto Broad Street in front of them. Emma's grip tightened on his arm. He heard her gasp. The little dog, its tail held high, threaded its way between cars moving in both directions, reached the opposite sidewalk and disappeared.

"Thank goodness," she said.

"I believe that's Buster—Judy Vines's dog. He's either very smart or very lucky."

"What would he be doing out at this hour?"

"How about picking up an order of take-out barbecue?"

Emma snorted. "Of course! Judy works at Bubba's Old-Fashioned Barbecue on Water Street."

"I can't say I blame Buster. They serve the best pulled pork in North Carolina."

"Are you thinking what I'm thinking?"

"Yeah, if we hang a right rather than a left on Stuart Lane, it's only two blocks to the top of Water Street. But aren't we a tad overdressed for a barbecue joint?"

"We wouldn't be if this was New York or Seattle."

"An excellent point. In fact, a day like I had today cries out for vinegar-based barbecue sauce rather than hollandaise."

"I agree," she said. "My day was bleak even before I showed up at your status briefing. I had a visit this morning from an antique broker. I've been trying to find a four-poster bed I can use to convert my one remaining single bedroom into a double."

Rafe nodded. Emma had begun to talk with a bubbly kind of enthusiasm he hadn't heard from her before.

She went on. "The broker had photos of a dozen antique four-posters—all of them too small, too big, too frilly, too expensive, or too flimsy."

"Too flimsy?"

"Guests are hard on furniture in a B and B."

"Ah."

"When she was ready to leave, she asked me, 'Isn't Glory the town where a bunch of kids put a Volkswagen on a B and B's porch?'"

"Naturally, you were standing on the very porch at the time."

"Dead center. But I didn't tell her that. Instead, I said, 'I'm amazed that you heard about that in Williamsburg, Virginia.'" Emma abruptly stopped walking. "Did I mention she was from Virginia?"

"No, but I figured it out. How did the lady respond to your amazement?"

"She said, 'Everyone who knows anything about B and Bs within five hundred miles has heard the story.' Then she wagged a bony finger at me. 'You folks in Glory had better nip that kind of thing in the bud. People who stay in B and Bs are conservative. They come for a splash of local color. They don't like to drown in it.'"

"What did you say to her?"

"Nothing. It doesn't pay to argue with SITs."

"SI—*whats?*"

"Self-important twits," she said, loudly.

"I like it. SIT is a delightful acronym. Can I steal it?"

"Feel free." Emma sighed. "The antique broker was my first SIT of the day. "Tyrone Keefe was my second."

"You argued with him."

"And you saw what a mistake that was. Anyway, my first SIT left me feeling gloomy, so I put on my sweats and vacuumed all the rooms that Peggy Lyons had just finished."

"Why?"

"Vacuuming cheers me up. It's a woman thing."

"Oh."

Rafe walked in silence for half a block. "A penny for your thoughts," Emma finally said.

"I was thinking about the B and B owners in Glory," he replied. "I'm impressed by your courage. You guys put everything at risk. Even a silly prank can threaten your future." He added, "I couldn't handle the stress."

"So you chose a low-stress career—police work."

"It's a different kind of stress."

"I'll say. How often do you deal with Tyrone Keefe?"

Rafe let himself smile. "Ty is a smart cop and hard to argue with. The Chief is beginning to agree with his interpretation of the evidence. I wish we had more leads."

Emma stopped again, this time under a streetlight on Water Street. Bubba's Barbecue was half a block away. Rafe fancied he could detect the smell of sauce wafting though the air.

"Well," she said, "there is one lead that we haven't considered yet."

To Rafe's surprise, Emma's "we" sounded perfectly appropriate. "You have my attention."

"There's some sort of connection between Lily Kirk and The Scottish Captain."

"Keep going."

"I told you that Lily planned to attend a meeting

of the Writing for Glory club at the Captain on Thursday evening."

"You did."

"But I didn't tell you that Lily asked me questions about the Captain the night before. She wanted to know if I was on duty twenty-four hours a day. She seemed pleased that I'd planned a trip to Elizabeth City on Thursday afternoon."

"Odd."

"It gets odder. Lily showed up when I was gone, convinced Hancock Jeffers that she had an appointment with me and spent about an hour alone in my front parlor. She left without a word before I got back."

Rafe considered the possibilities before he said, "It sounds to me that Lily wanted to be inside the Scottish Captain when she knew that you wouldn't be there."

"Exactly."

"But what would be her purpose?" Rafe asked. "Did she take anything?"

"Not that we can tell. Hancock checked pretty thoroughly."

"Then what was her visit for?"

Emma sighed. "I don't know, but I'll bet you another dinner that Lily had a good reason."

"You're on!"

Rafe suddenly realized that, win or lose, he would have another date with Emma.

He found himself enjoying the prospect immensely.

TWELVE

Emma smiled at Calvin Constable and said, "Have at it, Chef. Our one-and-only guest this week checked out an hour ago. I'm yours for the rest of the morning. Dazzle me with this year's holiday breakfast treat." She sniffed the air in the kitchen. "I do believe I'm going to enjoy it."

Calvin was sixtyish, slender, with thinning mouse-brown hair, matching eyes and a face that, Emma thought, would be impossible to describe if he ever disappeared. Everything about Calvin appeared "typical" to her. But put him in a kitchen and his features changed. His eyes became larger, his brows expressive, his nose seemed to twitch with anticipation as he fiddled with pans and measuring spoons.

"By the way," Emma added, "I love your new look." On this Tuesday morning, Calvin had donned a new white chef's tunic, a new plaid apron and an especially rakish new toque he had ordered from France. She made a mental note to remind Calvin to wear the same outfit when he toured the dining room each morning and greeted the guests.

Say it again with gusto. Bed-and-breakfast!

Calvin wiped his hands on the apron in the classic gesture of a master cook and used the stove as a backdrop for his presentation. "As in past years, Emma, I gave the matter of a new holiday breakfast dish much reflection. I also performed several experiments. My first notion was to develop a breakfast dish with a Christmas theme. I set out to create something memorable— a breakfast dish that sings of the Christmas season."

Emma wriggled in her desk chair to make herself more comfortable. If Calvin had a fault, it was long-windedness. He enjoyed expounding on his fabulous creations. Emma had decided a year earlier to allow Calvin as much showing-off time as he required. One didn't do anything to offend a chef of his caliber.

Calvin hailed from nearby Edenton, North Carolina. He had worked as a certified public accountant for the federal government in Washington, DC, for more than thirty-five years and retired back to Edenton. On a whim, he had signed up for the culinary technology program at a local community college. He graduated the same month that Emma had purchased The Scottish Captain. In an unmistakable example of God's providence, Calvin visited the Captain looking for a part-time cooking job—an opportunity to exercise his newly acquired skills—on the very morning that Emma had set aside to begin searching for a breakfast cook.

Calvin struck a pose of a man thinking. "What, I ask you, is more Christmassy then eggnog? So why not eggs poached in eggnog?"

After a few seconds of silence, Emma realized that Calvin expected her to answer his question. "*Hmm*—I don't know what to say. I've never heard of poaching anything in eggnog before."

"And you never will. It is impossible to keep boiling eggnog from curdling unless one adds *vast* quantities of brandy to the pot. That will hardly do at breakfast."

Emma bit her tongue. Two weeks earlier, Peggy Lyons had asked her about the peculiar-looking—and peculiar-smelling—"custard" that Calvin had thrown away.

He continued. "I immediately returned to the drawing board, so to speak. Perhaps the answer was to shift holidays. So, I invented a Thanksgiving Frittata made with eggs, turkey sausage, cranberries, chestnut stuffing and pumpkin puree."

"That sounds…*interesting*."

"You needn't be kind, Emma. My experimental frittata was an abject failure. Try to imagine Thanksgiving-dinner-flavored cat food."

"Yuck!"

"You have no idea! As I pushed the remains into the garbage disposal I prayed fervently, imploring God to ensure that my concoction did not injure Glory's waste treatment facility."

Emma laughed. Calvin resumed his tale. "Once more back to the drawing board, but this time I determined to stretch my creativity to the limit. I soon decided that an egg dish for the holidays need not have a holiday theme. The world has grown weary of *Oeufs à la Elf* and Pocahontas Quiche. Don't you agree?"

"I agree completely, Calvin. I have complete faith in your judgment. I often tell people that I trust you completely with a key component of my livelihood."

"Yes, well…" He began to blush. "I appreciate your confidence in me, and I assure you that it's well placed." He glanced at the timer atop the stove. "In precisely seventy-three seconds you will have the pleasure of sampling Scotch Eggs Capitán, a new breakfast dish that shall, I predict, become a staple at The Scottish Captain."

"Scotch Eggs Capitán...not Scotch Eggs Captain?" Emma said.

"I chose the Spanish variant of the word *captain* because my new creation is a fusion of both Mexican and Scottish influences."

"Now there's an unusual combination."

"Absolutely! But also a marriage of complementary tastes."

"I've had Scotch Eggs before," Emma said. "Hard-boiled eggs covered with a sausage meat shell."

"Scotch Eggs Capitán *expands* the simple concept. Picture a firm tomato shell with a thin outer sausage crust, filled with beaten eggs flavored with a bit of chili powder."

"Oh, boy. That sounds as delicious as it's beginning to smell." She sniffed the air again.

"Indeed, it is delicious. The only question left is this—do we serve it on a tortilla or atop a Scottish scone?"

Emma's head turned as the timer beeped. "They're ready!"

Calvin carried a steaming baking sheet from the oven and set it on a trivet in the center of Emma's desk. She studied the six round sausage-covered spheres, each with a puff of baked egg poking through the top.

"They're beautiful," she said. "We could serve them on corn bread rounds, perhaps with a dollop of guacamole or sour cream."

"Stop gilding the lily and try one." He used two serving spoons to move the largest of the Scotch Eggs Capitán to a plate. Emma attacked it with knife and fork, then took a bite.

"Scrumptious, delectable, delicious and luscious," she said. "I can picture you on the cover of *Gourmet* magazine holding a plateful of Scotch Eggs Capitán."

A gentle tap-tapping on the back door interrupted Emma's tribute.

Calvin craned his neck to look out the window. "A teenage girl wearing a cheerleader jacket and a gold-and-white scarf. Red hair. Quite good looking."

Emma pushed her chair away from the desk and stood up. "That sounds like Kate Neilson. But it can't be Kate…." She moved to the door and turned the knob.

"Kate!" Emma felt herself frown. "Is anything wrong? You're supposed to be in school at this hour."

Kate unwound her long scarf. "I decided to be late for my first class this morning. It's no big deal. I have a perfect attendance record and I'm getting an A in English. Can I come in?"

"Of course." Emma opened the door wide.

"We need to talk." Kate glanced uncomfortably at Calvin. "Alone, if you don't mind."

Before Emma could respond, Calvin said, "As it happens, I have a telephone call to make. Why don't I go to the office near the parlor and leave you two alone for perhaps ten minutes?"

Emma acknowledged his kindness with a wink. "What do we need to talk about?" she asked Kate, after Calvin had left.

"My father, of course. It's high time we had a woman-to-woman chat."

"I see." Emma studied Kate's face for any sign of sarcasm or pretense. The girl seemed utterly sincere. Emma gestured toward a stool next to her desk. "Have a seat."

As Kate perched on a stool she spotted the pan full of Scotch Eggs Capitán. "What are those?"

"A new breakfast dish that my chef invented. Want to try one?"

"Sure."

Emma retrieved another plate and served Kate a sausage-wrapped tomato. "They're called Scotch Eggs Capitán. Now, let's talk about Rafe."

Kate nodded slowly. "I'd appreciate knowing your intentions toward him."

Emma stared at Kate. *My intentions?* Emma's brain abruptly ceased to work. She struggled to come up with a coherent thought but couldn't. Kate rescued her. "I'm doing this backward," she said. "I should apologize to you first."

"*Uh*...apologize for what?" Emma asked.

"The other day, I insulted you behind your back. I told Dad you're a loser." Kate deftly carved her Scotch Egg Capitán into several bite-sized pieces with the edge of her fork. "When I said that, I didn't know that you were a successful businesswoman before you moved to Glory. Now I think you're cool."

"May I ask what changed your mind about me?"

"I looked you up on Google and printed out the stuff I found, including pictures of you with lots of famous people who stayed at your hotel. I especially like the photos of you shaking hands with movie stars."

"Consider yourself forgiven." Emma looked away, not sure whether to laugh or scream. "May I ask a follow-up question? What makes you think I have *intentions* about your father?"

"For starters, you've been spending all kinds of time with him. It's also totally obvious to me that he likes you. His face gets all glowy when he talks about you. He thinks you're smart."

Emma felt a spark of excitement. *Glowy* was a good word to describe her recent reactions to Rafe.

Don't jump to conclusions. He hasn't said or done anything to indicate how he feels about you.

"I'll be honest, Kate. I'm helping your dad look into Lily Kirk's recent car accident. That's the chief reason you've seen us together so often."

Kate's face darkened. "I don't want to talk about Lily Kirk. My dad keeps asking me questions. I keep telling him that the Phantom Avenger had nothing to do with the accident, but I don't think he believes me."

Emma shuddered as a chill gripped her insides. All at once she understood why Rafe had been trying so hard to prove the existence of another Phantom Avenger. *He fears that Kate may be involved in Lily's death.* Rafe had often talked about teenagers, high school students and Contemporaries, but Emma had never made the obvious connection between Kate Neilson and the series of pranks that seem to culminate with Lily's car wreck.

This girl can't be involved. I won't believe it, either.

"The only reason I mentioned the accident, Kate," Emma said, "is that it helps explain my relationship with your father. We've become professional colleagues, so to speak."

"This breakfast is delicious. I haven't had anything like it before." She took a big bite of Scotch Egg Capitán.

"I'll convey your compliments to the chef."

"I also think you're lying about my father."

"What?"

"You like him a lot. You look at him the same way he looks at you."

Emma, struck tongue-tied again, could only gawk. Kate went on. "I want you to know that I've changed my mind about you. It's okay if you want to marry Dad. I withdraw all my objections."

"Ah…

Kate slipped off the stool. "Before I forget. Can I see the metal softball?"

"Pardon?"

"One of the stories I read on the Internet says that your team in Seattle bronzed the softball you used during the last inning of the championship."

Emma marveled at Kate's fast-changing mental tracks. "The softball is in the parlor on the bookshelf near the window."

Kate immediately headed for the parlor.

"Wow," she said. "Is it heavy?"

"Take it out of its wooden stand and see."

Kate lifted the ball gingerly. "It's not much heavier than a plain softball."

"Nope. Bronzing adds a thin layer of bronze plating to the outside of the ball."

Kate carefully replaced the ball on its stand. She smiled at Emma and said, "You're cool and hot at the same time. There aren't many of us around."

"Ah…thanks."

As Emma led Kate back to the kitchen, the girl said, "I need to ask you a big favor. Don't tell Dad that I came to see you today."

"Okay."

"Promise?"

Emma drew her finger across her chest. "Cross my heart."

Kate nodded with obvious satisfaction and moved to the back door. "Thank you." She paused in the open doorway. "You have to make your own decision, but keep in mind that cool guys like Dad don't come along every day."

Emma mumbled, "I know that. He's the coolest guy in Glory."

What am I saying?

Kate had shut the door before Emma could take back her ridiculous words. Even worse, she had been left speechless by a high school freshman who had posed a straightforward question: What were her intentions toward Rafe Neilson?

The problem is—you don't want to admit how you feel.

Rafe looked at the list that Angie Ringgold had put together.

"She may have visited other businesses in town," Angie said, "but those are the only three where people definitely remember Lily Kirk."

"Good job."

He looked at his clock—ten after two—and reached for his telephone.

"This is The Scottish Captain. Good afternoon."

"Can I interest you in another field trip?"

"I suppose so. My time is my own this afternoon. Where are we going?"

"Glory Stationery and Office Supply... The Glory Book Nook...and Glory National Bank. In that order."

"Why?"

"You got me thinking about Lily last night. We know that she visited The Scottish Captain for an hour on Thursday afternoon, and we know that she went off to a hobby shop in Elizabeth City after that. But what did she do the rest of the day? I asked Angie Ringgold to phone every business in Glory and ask whether Lily stopped by on Thursday morning. Angie had three hits." He added, "I'll pick you up in ten minutes."

"Well…"

"It's too late for second thoughts. You've agreed to join me."

"What are you going to say if someone wants to know why I'm tagging along with you?"

"I'll figure that out when someone asks. Anyway, chances are nobody will take notice of you unless you begin to talk. You watch and listen—I'll do all the questioning."

Rafe heard Emma sigh. "Okay, you're the expert."

He found Emma waiting for him on Broad Street in front of the Captain. She looked especially lovely in a bright red coat and tartan scarf. He scurried around the Corvette and opened the passenger door for her. "Onward to Glory Stationery and Office Supply," she said, as she climbed in.

Rafe drove to MacTavish Street on the north end of town. The shop was one of six in an old warehouse building that had been converted into a small strip mall. He found a parking spot directly in front of the tinted plate-glass door. A heavyset woman in her forties, with Jean Harlow–colored blond hair, waved at him when he followed Emma inside.

"Hi, Selma," he said.

"Hi, Rafe. Angie told me you might drop by today." Selma smiled at Emma. "You're Emma McCall. I've seen you at Chamber of Commerce meetings."

"And you're Selma Douglas, right?"

"As rain. I'll be with you as soon as I dispose of my *non*customer here."

"Actually, Emma is with me," Rafe said.

Selma Douglas frowned. Rafe could almost hear her unasked question reverberating through the shop: *Why is Emma McCall with you?*

He glanced at Emma, who was peering up at the ceiling, doing her best to smile innocently and say nothing.

"Ms. McCall is participating in our 'ride along' program," he said matter-of-factly. "She's an observer, learning how the Glory Police Department operates."

"Really?" Selma's frown became a sly smirk. "Who do I call? I'd like to volunteer next month."

Rafe changed the subject. "Did Angie tell you what I'm after?"

"You want to know why Lily Kirk shopped here last Thursday morning."

"That would be most helpful. What did she buy?"

Selma removed her eyeglasses and let them fall to her chest and dangle from a gold chain around her neck. "She didn't buy a thing, more's the pity. We had exactly what she wanted."

"Which was?"

"A magnifying glass." She moved to a shelf behind the main counter and retrieved a cardboard box. "This is the only model we stock. Rigid aluminum frame, a top-quality lens made in Austria and a built-in light." She clicked a switch. "Nifty, isn't it? Fifty-three dollars plus tax."

Rafe lifted the magnifier and studied the top of his

left hand. The pores and wrinkles became horrifyingly clear. "Powerful." He returned the magnifier to its box. "What didn't Lily like about it?"

"The price. She wanted a magnifier that cost less than ten dollars." Selma sniffed. "I sent her off to Elizabeth City. The hobby shop on the main drag has a large selection of cheap magnifiers. Not my cup of tea, of course, but many people are willing to settle for less than the best."

"Do you remember at what time Lily came in?"

"Right after we opened up. It must have been a few minutes after nine-thirty."

"Did she tell you why she wanted a magnifying glass?"

"Not exactly, but I figure it had something to do with books. She was carrying one under her arm when she came in and she looked at one of the pages with a magnifier."

"Do you remember the name of the book?"

"Sorry, but I never saw the name. Lily moved sideways so that I couldn't get a look at the title. I guess she wanted to keep it a secret." Selma put her glasses back on. "Are you going to tell me what this is all about?"

"There's not much to tell. We found a magnifying glass in Lily's car. I was curious where it came from. Thanks to you, now I know."

Soon after Rafe turned south on King Street, Emma said, "I'm impressed—you told her the truth, but you didn't reveal any significant information."

"It's an art form," he replied. "It took me years to master."

She responded with a laugh, a joyous tinkle that Rafe thought delightful. There was no need, he decided, to share the thought that was dampening his own amusement. If Glory Stationery had stocked a low-cost magnifier, Lily might not have driven to Elizabeth City. She wouldn't have blown her horn in "the forest primeval" and sent the Taurus hurtling off the road.

"But the murderer would have found another time and place to kill her," he muttered.

"What did you say?" Emma asked.

"Not a thing."

"You're not much of a conversationalist today."

"Driving around Glory doesn't give you much time to converse. We've just driven clear across town—and there's Osborn Street."

Rafe pulled into a parking lot alongside a three-story redbrick building that had once housed Glory's first drugstore. The Glory Book Nook was on the second floor. He guided Emma to the front of the building, through a narrow doorway and up a steep flight of steps.

Rafe began to smell the bookstore at the top of the stairs. The air in the hallway outside seemed heavy with dust and the moldy paper smell of old books. He fought back a sneeze then pushed open the glass paneled front door. Somewhere inside a signal bell rang.

"Feel free to browse," Sam Lange called from somewhere in the back of the shop."

"It's me, Sam," Rafe called back, "Rafe Neilson."

"Oh, yeah. Angie Ringgold said to expect you. Be right there."

Sam appeared a few seconds later. This time, Rafe didn't wait for a confused reaction to his companion. "Emma McCall is on a 'ride along' with me today. She's observing how the department works."

"I didn't know we had a 'ride along' program in Glory."

"It's relatively new."

Emma's right. You are quick with a fib. Rafe realized that he hadn't had to lie to anyone since he moved to Glory, but then this was his first murder investigation.

Everyone stretches the truth when the crime is homicide. Why shouldn't the police have the same privilege?

"You told Angie that Lily Kirk visited you on Thursday morning."

Sam nodded. "She came in about ten."

"You recall what she wanted?"

"I think mostly to talk. She began by telling me that she wasn't quite ready to deliver the next batch of books that had been recovered from the Caruthers's attic, but that she might have them for me by the weekend."

"What did Lily do with the books before she gave them to you?"

"She estimated a value for each volume, usually by checking its price at three different Internet book dealers. Valuing one book at a time is a tedious process, but we couldn't figure out a simpler way to meet the requirements of the Caruthers bequest."

Sam shrugged. "I told her not to hurry, that I really didn't care if she was a week late delivering them. Most of the books she'd given me before were junk—old volumes with hardly any value." He frowned. "That's when she began to cry."

"Cry?" Rafe asked. "About what?"

"Lily said that she felt terrible bringing me so many worthless books…that it wasn't fair…that John Caruthers was stupid for doing what he did." He shook his head. "She went off in a dozen different directions. I didn't even try to keep track of her meanderings. I figured she was in a bad mood and just needed someone who would listen."

"So you listened?"

"Uh-huh," Sam said, "I also made her a cup of tea."

"And?"

"She pretended to snap out of her rotten mood. She began to smile, but I could tell she was faking. She told me not to pay any attention to her, that she was having trouble sleeping. I figured that lack of sleep explained her flaky behavior. She gave me a kiss on my cheek and went on her way."

"You said she arrived at ten o'clock. When did she leave?"

"Maybe ten-thirty. Maybe a few minutes later." Sam grimaced. "I never saw her again." He averted his eyes. "Do you think I made a mistake letting her drive in such an upset frame of mind? I could have tried to stop her from leaving. I could have insisted that she at least talk to Reverend Hartman."

Rafe clapped Sam on his shoulder. "Trust me, nothing you could have done would have changed what happened to Lily Kirk." Rafe spoke with all the sincerity he could muster, but he could see that Sam Lange didn't buy any of it.

Give me a few more days, Sam, and we'll figure out who's responsible for Lily's death.

"Perhaps you should stay in the car when we get to the bank." Rafe quickly added, "They tend to be a persnickety bunch. I doubt they'll be willing to tell me anything unless I produce a court order."

"I understand, concur with and applaud your decision. The reek of old books almost did me in on our last stop. I'm thrilled to stay outdoors and breathe fresh air."

Rafe turned right on Main Street. The granite Glory National Bank building—the biggest building in town—lay ahead on the northeast corner of the Front and Main intersection. He parked the Corvette on Front Street and left the engine running.

"Goodness!" Emma said. "You actually trust me with your Number One toy."

Rafe began to grin. "Now that you mention it, I suppose I do."

"I'll practice shifting when you're gone. I never learned to drive a car with a manual transmission."

He felt his grin become a grimace. *"What?"*

"I'm joking. Go!"

Rafe enjoyed walking through Glory National Bank because he loved the sound of his leather soles clicking against the bank's marble floor. He made for a tiny office in the back of the bank. Its occupant, Doris Paisley, the assistant manager, was expecting him.

After they exchanged hellos, she said, "Angie told me you were conducting some sort of investigation. That strikes me as an odd thing to do after a routine traffic accident."

"I'm investigating a suspicious death," he replied. "When I'm sure it's a routine traffic accident, I'll stop my investigation."

Doris made a soft whistle. "Well, well, well. Who woulda thunk it?"

"That's between you and me."

"Understood, although I hope you're not going to ask me to divulge any of the details of Lily Kirk's account with us."

"Nary a one. What I need to know is why she visited the bank last Thursday."

She seemed to relax. "That I can talk about. Lily asked about our safety-deposit boxes, but we had none available in the size she needed."

"What size did she ask for?"

"Our biggest." She gestured with her hands. "Ten inches high, ten inches deep, twenty-four inches long. Lily wanted to rent two of them."

"Did she say why she needed two boxes that large?"

Doris fingered the single strand of pearls at her neck. "I didn't ask, and she didn't tell—but I admit that I thought it unusual. Our largest boxes cost three hundred dollars a year. Few individuals rent even one, unless they own valuable stamp or coin collections."

"What time did Lily come in?"

"Sometime around eleven-thirty. After I finished with her, I went to lunch."

Rafe walked back to the Corvette wondering what valuables Lily owned that would require *two* jumbo safe-deposit boxes. Equally important, where were the valuables now?

He climbed into the driver's seat and posed the problem to Emma.

"*Two* boxes?" she said. "That makes no sense."

He released the brake and slipped the Corvette into gear. "I'll bet it will after we figure out who killed Lily."

"Why do you say that?"

He accelerated and turned west on Campbell Street. "Because I have a gut feeling that Doris Paisley handed us the key to unlocking the case."

He turned left on Broad Street.

"Where are we going?" Emma asked.

"To The Scottish Captain. I'll take you home, then

head back to Police Headquarters. I want to read my e-mail."

"Forget about your e-mail! You're not going anywhere until we've talked about the stuff we learned today."

"Do you have an alternative plan in mind?"

"You bet. We crank up the coffee-pod machine at the Captain. I get to pick your brain until you have to go home to your daughter."

Rafe chuckled. "Sounds fair to me."

And you get to spend more time with Emma.

Why didn't you think of it?

THIRTEEN

"I hope you don't mind drinking your coffee in the kitchen," Emma said to Rafe as she led him up the Captain's broad porch steps. "Because I don't have any guests this week, I've turned the heat down in much of the building. The only really comfortable room on the first floor is the kitchen."

Rafe smiled. "The kitchen will be fine, as long as you promise not to yell at me."

Emma winced with embarrassment as she remembered the last time Rafe had been in her kitchen. It had been on the day that the Phantom Avenger moved the Volkswagen Bug onto the porch. She'd been thoroughly inhospitable to him—*twice.* She'd encouraged him to leave as quickly as possible; essentially ordered him out of the building. Today was different. Today she relished inviting him into her home. She felt a flutter of excitement when she realized how dramatically her feelings had changed.

Does he feel the same way about you?

She unlocked the Captain's front door and stepped inside. Rafe followed close behind her. He hung his duty jacket on the empty coatrack.

"Wait here a minute. I'll get the pod coffeemaker."

Emma detoured into the rear parlor and unplugged the appliance. When she returned to the hallway, Rafe said, "It *is* cold in here." He sounded surprised and his face had filled with concern. "I finally get it. You *really* are without guests." He added quickly, "When do they come back?"

"Two couples will check in on Sunday evening. I'm completely booked for the Thanksgiving weekend and Christmas week. With luck I'll pick up some last-minute reservations."

"And that's enough business to keep the owner of The Scottish Captain a happy camper?"

"I even hope to make a small profit this year."

"That's nice to hear."

"Assuming, of course, that the negative publicity that Glory received doesn't translate into a flood of cancellations."

"We'll make sure that it doesn't." Rafe abruptly looked up at the ceiling. "What's the whining sound I hear?"

"Hancock Jeffers is refinishing the sink stand in one of the upstairs bathrooms."

"Excellent."

Excellent? Emma stared at Rafe. Since when had he become interested in routine maintenance? A trickle of comprehension grew into a flood of understanding. *Rafe cares about the Captain because he cares about me.*

She sensed her heart had begun to race, and she felt unsure of what to say or do next. She backed through the swinging door that led to the kitchen and switched on the ceiling light.

You want him to care, don't you?

Now that was the question that needed answering. Her divorce from Charlie represented a kind of line in the sand. She had become a devoted businessperson; there would be no new relationships with men, at least not until she'd transformed The Scottish Captain into the most successful bed-and-breakfast in North Carolina.

But Rafe Neilson had arrived in her life unexpectedly. Did he change the rules? And if so, what were her new priorities?

She sighed as she plugged in the pod coffeemaker.

Rafe came through the swinging door and said, "I've had a brainstorm about Lily Kirk's last day that I want to bounce off you."

"Bounce away!" she said, brightly.

Hooray. Chatting with Rafe is so much more pleasant than brooding about Charlie—even if we're discussing a murder.

He perched on a kitchen stool. "Everything seemed to go wrong for Lily last Thursday. She couldn't find an economical magnifier in Glory…she didn't deliver books to Sam Lange…the bank didn't have any large safe-deposit boxes to rent…and whatever reason she had to visit the Captain, well that seems to have gone south, too."

"I've had days like that."

"Do you know which of the errands troubles me most? Her trip to The Glory Book Nook. She told Sam Lange that she wasn't ready to deliver his boxes of books, but she had them with her—in her car's trunk—later that evening. How did that happen?"

"Obviously, she went home sometime during the day and loaded them in her car."

"But when did she have the time to do the valuations? Remember, she estimated the value of each book individually. Most of her day was taken up with the three errands, sitting in your parlor, then driving to Elizabeth City."

"Good point," Emma said. "But that would mean..."

Rafe jumped in. "That's what I think, too. She had the books in her car all day. But for some reason, she didn't want to deliver them to Sam."

"How does French Vanilla Mocha Blend sound?" Emma asked, as the water in the coffee-pod machine began to bubble.

"Froufrou, but tasty."

The "ready" light blinked on. She laughed and pushed Brew.

"What about Lily's other errands?" Emma said. "Anything troubling about them?"

"Not to me. Lily seems to have wanted a cheap magnifying glass and a pair of safe-deposit boxes."

"There's a thought. Maybe she visited the Captain to borrow a magnifying glass?"

"Or your safe-deposit box."

Emma opened the refrigerator and brought out half of a cinnamon coffee cake that Calvin had stored in a plastic container. The translucent plastic box caught her attention.

Lily wanted a safe-deposit box. But maybe she settled for...

"Penny for your thoughts," Rafe asked.

"Well, your wisecrack about borrowing our safe-deposit box got me thinking. There's supposed to be a lost hidden compartment, a money safe, somewhere in this building."

Rafe, suddenly alert, said, "No one knows where it is?"

Emma smiled. "That's why it's considered 'lost,' although I'm certain it's not on the second or third floor. Carole and Duncan Frasier did major renovations on two and three when they bought the place in 1982.

Duncan was fascinated by the tales of a secret compartment. He looked hard and would have found it." She didn't explain that the Frasiers had never gotten around to finishing the third floor, and that the Captain's so-called owner's apartment was still a work in progress.

"Would Lily have known about the money safe?"

"Sure. The Scottish Captain's secret compartment is famous. It's been written about in travel guides for tourists."

"Do you think Lily knew how to find it?"

"I don't see how...*except*...this building was used as a boardinghouse during the 1950s and 1960s. I suppose it's possible that if Lily stayed here awhile she might have discovered the money safe's location."

Rafe shook his head. "We're building speculation atop speculation, a dangerous thing to do. How do we find out if Lily Kirk spent any time in this building?"

"We simply look in a book," Emma said. "The old guest register is in my front parlor."

Rafe slid off his stool. "Show me."

Emma led Rafe to the front parlor to an antique mahogany bookcase that stood next to the front window. "It's that big leather-bound journal on the top shelf."

Rafe retrieved the oversize book and read the title embossed on its front cover. "'*Rooms Of Glory*,' a tad pretentious, if you ask me." He began to flip through the pages. "Here she is. Lily Kirk moved in on June 15, 1979, and stayed here through April, 1982. She lived at Rooms of Glory for almost three years."

"Right up until the Frasiers bought the building and transformed it into The Scottish Captain."

"The timing makes sense. That's about when Lily's mother's worsening illness forced the sale of her house.

The house was sold, Mom went to a nursing home and daughter moved to Rooms of Glory."

"Three years is a long time. More than enough, I'd wager, to discover the location of the secret money safe."

"Wanna know what I think?" Rafe slammed the leather-bound journal shut.

"First, Lily did know where to find your secret compartment.

"Second, she visited the Captain last Thursday to hide some sort of valuable objects. She couldn't rent a large safe-deposit box, so she decided to use your money safe, evidently out of desperation."

"I don't think so." Emma could barely keep her excitement in check. "Lily didn't come here out of desperation. *The Captain was her Plan B.*"

"I get it! Her preference was a pair of safe-deposit boxes, but she had a backup ready."

Emma threw her hand up in a gesture of elation. "It all fits! Lily reacted with concern when I told her I'd refurbished some of the first floor. She was worried that I might have destroyed the secret compartment. She also seemed remarkably happy when I told her about my planned trip to Elizabeth City."

"So, what did Lily hide, and where is the money safe?"

"I don't know, and I don't know, but as long as we're still speculating, let me offer a new guess. I think that the person who killed Lily subsequently broke into her town house expecting to find the valuable objects. Of course, they weren't there because Lily had hidden them—" Emma spun around once "—somewhere in the Captain, in our fabled secret compartment."

Rafe grinned at her. "You've just accounted for the

damage done inside Lily's town house. The person in question must have become furious, because now he or she has no way to find the valuable objects. The only person who knew where she put them is dead."

"But that means…" Emma paused to choose her next words carefully.

"What does it mean?"

Emma spoke softly and deliberately. "We can use The Scottish Captain as bait to catch the killer. All we have to do is spread the word—cleverly, of course—that Lily visited the Captain a few hours before she died."

"Absolutely not!" Rafe spoke with more determination than Emma had heard from him before. "No clever traps, no games designed to lure a killer."

"All I'm suggesting…" Emma began.

"I understand what you're suggesting. I won't let you play dangerous games."

"Where's the danger?"

Rafe put his hands on her shoulders. "The danger lies in our lack of knowledge. We don't know anything about our 'person in question.' You hunt a grizzly bear differently than you hunt a fox. Otherwise you run the risk of getting eaten. We're not ready to set traps yet because we don't know who we're trying to catch."

Emma pushed away from Rafe. "Okay, I get your message." She took a breath to calm her annoyance. "No traps until we understand our quarry better."

"Thank you for being reasonable."

"Let's go back to the kitchen and have our coffee and cake."

He smiled at her. "Let's."

Emma let Rafe lead the way. She watched him plod toward the kitchen.

That's the problem with policemen. They have limited imaginations. They don't recognize a great idea when they hear one.

Rafe glanced at the dark sky and wondered why it seemed so threatening.

Because one of your basic premises might be wrong.

What if the person who killed Lily Kirk *also* knows about Lily's connection to The Scottish Captain? What if the killer guesses that Lily hid the valuable objects somewhere on the Captain's first floor?

The objects had sufficient value to be a motive for Lily Kirk's murder. Rafe doubted that the murderer would hesitate to kill Emma McCall to get them.

He hated the idea of Emma being alone tonight in that big house. Before driving away, he'd walked the perimeter of the property. Everything seemed secure; all the doors and windows were locked.

Rafe had also asked Sergeant Myer, the policeman on overnight duty, to check the Captain every half hour or so. He also prayed for Emma's safety. "Dear Lord, I thank You for your providence that keeps the people of Glory safe. I lift up Your servant Emma Kirk tonight. Please watch over her and protect her from harm. In Jesus's name, I pray."

Rafe had gone to bed in a nervous mood, half-expecting his telephone to wake him in the middle of the night. He slept fitfully and finally gave up trying at five o'clock. He drove past The Scottish Captain himself at five-thirty and again at six. At seven he dialed her number on his cell phone.

"The Scottish Captain."

"You sound happy."

"I am happy. I went to bed feeling that all was well. I slept like the proverbial baby. How about you?"

Emma seemed to have forgotten the outburst of unpleasantness that had unsettled the evening before. Moreover, she'd begun today in a fine mood. Rafe chose his answer carefully. If he spelled out his concerns he might sound like a world-class worrywart. "I slept well, too." He quickly switched to a new topic. "What are your plans for today?"

"I've lined up a dozen different maintenance chores to do. They'll keep me busy right up to choir practice this evening. I'll see you at church." She hung up before he could object.

His own day went quickly, given over to administrative duties—mostly budget and salary related—that took his mind off the possible location of hidden money safes at The Scottish Captain. He did, however, raise the issue with Angie Ringgold during a coffee break.

"You're a native of Glory, right?" Rafe said.

"Born and bred."

"What do you know about the money safes and secret compartments that are reputed to exist within Glory's older homes?"

She shrugged. "Only what I've read in the travel guides. They were used to store money and valuables before Glory had a bank. Some folks claim that they came in handy during Prohibition to hide moonshine liquor."

"Say I wanted to find one. Where would I look?"

Angie shrugged again. "Beats me. Some of the designs are supposed to be really clever. You can look forever and not find them."

"On that grim note," he muttered to himself, "I'll get back to work."

Rafe arrived at Glory Community Church at a few minutes before seven. He heard Emma talking before he saw her.

"I could kick myself for not pressing Lily for more details, but I always assumed that the so-called secret money safe in The Scottish Captain was a legend. In fact, I told Lily that the night before her terrible accident. She assured me that there was a secret compartment in the Captain and that she knew where it was."

Rafe felt the color drain from his face. Had Emma gone mad? What game was she playing? Why had she broken her promise?

Emma was surrounded by more than half of the choir. A few steps away, Daniel Hartman, Nina McEwen and Sara Knoll—all sipping from cans of soda—were listening intently.

"Why didn't you ask her where you could find the secret compartment?" Debbie asked.

"I did," Emma said, "but Lily refused to tell me. She said that she wanted me to have the same kind of fun that she did when she searched for it almost thirty years ago. As I understand it, Lily lived at the old Rooms of Glory boardinghouse in the months before her mother died. That's when she was able to search for and find the money safe."

"That doesn't surprise me at all. Lily was quite a history buff," Sam Lange said. "She was also very kind-hearted. If you had asked her again to lead you to the secret compartment, I think she would have."

"Funny you should say that," Emma said. "Lily tried to visit me at The Scottish Captain a few hours before her accident. I was in Elizabeth City, so I didn't get to see her. I'll bet that she wanted to show me the secret compartment."

Rafe scanned the people in the room. Was Lily's killer one of them? It was certainly a good possibility. Lily traveled in a small circle, without many friends. Her church family might well include a traitor.

Some might find it hard to believe that a cold-blooded killer would also sing in a church choir, but Rafe felt sure it had happened many times before. Singing hymns didn't erase the most common reasons for murder: greed, lust, revenge and fear.

Rafe tried to estimate the effect of Emma's words on a killer, should one be present. Would Emma be seen as a threat? Would she become the killer's next target?

"But you did get to meet with Lily the night before she died?" Lane Johnson asked.

Emma nodded. "I consider myself fortunate to have had an opportunity to spend some quality time with Lily. She took me to Dan's Pizza Deluxe, out on Route 34A. We ate poppers and talked about many things."

"What kinds of *things?*" Phoebe Hecht said.

Rafe mouthed a silent prayer. *Lord, please don't let her answer that.*

"Lily was actually quite upset that evening," Emma began. "She'd had a frightening experience on the highway…"

Rafe smiled at Phoebe, "Emma has a creative imagination. Sometimes she lets it run wild."

Emma frowned at him. "Don't be silly, Rafe, I'm not imagining anything. Lily and I sat together at a small table. I know exactly what she said."

Rafe thought about grabbing Emma by the arm and propelling her out of the choir practice room before she could say any more. But how would he explain himself to the others? And would Emma ever forgive him?

Emma went on. "She told me that a pickup truck had tried to push her car off the road that afternoon."

Michelle Engle gasped. "And a day later, she had a fatal accident?"

"If it really was an *accident,*" Candy Cole said.

"You know, you're right," Phoebe said. "I never did like the idea that Lily's hood bounced up accidentally and caused her to run off the road."

"I agree!" Michelle said. "It's much more likely that someone helped things along, someone who didn't want Lily around anymore." She cast an ugly look at Tony Taylor, Judy Vines and Sam Lange.

"Wait a minute!" Tony boomed. "Are you suggesting that the Contemporaries are responsible for Lily's death?"

"Who else wanted her out of the picture?" Candy said. "Who else would benefit from the death of a middle-aged woman? Lily was the leader of the Traditionalists. Eliminate her and you just might win the battle."

"That's nonsense!" Sam said. "Our *battle,* as you call it, is a trivial dispute inside a small church, inside a small town in North Carolina. You make it sound like we're fighting World War III." He stood tall. "Besides, Lily Kirk was a friend of mine. We both love books. A bond that strong doesn't get broken over the question of what kind of music to play on Sunday."

"Nice words," Michelle said, "but hollow. You people turned this into a major fight when you invented the Phantom Avenger."

"An excellent point!" Phoebe said. She turned to Rafe. "What do the police have to say? Are you going to investigate the possibility that Lily died as a result of a stupid prank?"

Rafe's mind raced. It was a perfectly valid question but also the absolutely last question he wanted to answer. "You have my word, Dr. Hecht, that the Glory Police Department will investigate every possibility related to the death of Ms. Kirk."

"You can't believe that we are involved." Debbie Akers moved slowly toward Rafe. "You know that Kate and I and the other kids wouldn't hurt anyone, especially not Lily Kirk." She looked up at Rafe, her eyes pleading. "Say that you believe me." Before he could say anything, Debbie whirled around and ran from the church.

Rafe felt his shoulders sag. Everything he had worked to keep private was now public. Did Emma realize the problems she had created for Kate?

All at once, the yelling escalated. The Contemporaries and Traditionalists created a cacophony of insults, claims and counterclaims. Nina McEwen, tears welling in her eyes and a look of horror on her face, moved from person to person trying to stop the fight, to no avail.

Amidst the screaming, Rafe heard a gentle sobbing behind him. He turned. Emma McCall, alone and ashen-faced, was slowly backing out of the choir practice room.

She looked into his eyes. "I, I didn't mean to do this."

He smiled the best he could. "I know you didn't."

Daniel Hartman's thunderous military voice filled the room. "Go home, everyone. Nina will try to schedule a new rehearsal for Saturday."

"What have I done?" Emma said, to no one and everyone.

Before Rafe could stop her she bolted through the door. For a terrible moment, he wondered if he should let her go.

FOURTEEN

Emma ran out of Glory Community Church without looking back. The choir was mad at her, the pastor was mad at her, Rafe Neilson was mad at her. Even more important, she was mad at herself.

Impetuous, overconfident and stupid Emma McCall. The woman who acts before she thinks. The woman who made Nina McEwen cry once again.

Poor Nina! Less than two months to Christmas, and her singers are in another uproar. Well, that will teach her to let someone in the choir who isn't a member of the church.

Emma trotted east on Oliver Street for a block, then slowed her pace to a fast walk. This wasn't the way home, but she didn't feel ready to return to The Scottish Captain—at least not yet. She needed to calm down, she especially needed to think. A brisk walk would give her the chance to do both.

Along with another opportunity to enjoy Glory's small-town ambience.

Even in the dark, the town's old houses looked inviting, soft light filtering through the curtained windows. She sniffed the air and smelled hickory. Someone was burning the expensive hardwood in a fireplace. The sweet fragrance reminded her that winter, such as it was here in the South, had almost arrived.

When they ride you out of town on a rail, try to find an equally charming place to live with an equally moderate climate.

She heard footsteps coming up behind her and moved aside to let the person pass. A familiar voice announced: "You forgot to turn south onto Broad Street."

"I suppose you've come to gloat," she said, without looking at Rafe. "To say I told you so."

"Nope. I've come to watch your back."

She accelerated to a speed walk. "Leave me alone, Rafe, I'm in a rotten mood."

"As well you should be." He added, "Where are you going?"

"I have no idea. Does it really make any difference?"

"Well, if you keep walking at your current pace in your current direction, you'll be swimming in Albemarle Sound in roughly three minutes."

"Fancy that. I learn something new every day." She glanced at him over her shoulder. "How did you find me in the dark?"

"If you want to disappear at night, don't wear a bright red coat."

"Good point." She added, "Why does my back need watching?"

"Because you may have cleverly told a killer that Lily stashed valuable objects somewhere inside The Scottish Captain."

"Not so cleverly. My clumsiness wrecked one of the best church choirs in eastern North Carolina."

"No, that deed had been done by the Caruthers

bequest long before you put on your little act. The Traditionalists and the Contemporaries have been battling for the past six months. You rattled their cages at choir practice, that's all."

"I also ignored your direct order not to set a trap for the killer."

"Yes, I'm curious about that. Why did you go blazing ahead, despite my helpful advice?"

"Because this alleged investigation of ours—*sorry, yours*—is mired in quicksand. Because there was no way you could keep Kate and the other high school kids out of the spotlight. Because I rarely think my ideas through before I speak. Because I can be impulsive and pea brained. Are those enough reasons?"

"They'll do for a start." He reached for her hand and moved close to her side. "Nothing you did at church qualifies as a capital offense. However, you may have placed yourself in considerable danger."

"Not in the short run. The only danger I face tonight is the risk of putting my foot even deeper into my mouth than I did this evening."

"It must have left an awful taste. How about a cup of coffee to cleanse your palate?"

Emma pulled her hand free. "You're inviting me for coffee after the mess I've made?"

"For coffee and also to decide what we do next. You've certainly given Lily's killer something to think about."

"I hope so, although it will take a while for word of that to seep out to the general community and reach the responsible person."

"Unless the killer is a member of the Glory Community Choir."

She stopped walking. "That's not possible."

"Oh, it's possible, maybe even probable. Lily didn't travel in large circles. The choir represents the single biggest group of people she hung out with."

"But a church choir is like *family.*"

"The family is where most murders happen."

Emma felt herself shiver. "I'm suddenly cold. Where can we get that cup of coffee you offered?"

"My house is only two blocks away."

"Your house…"

"If you're worried about Kate, don't be. As of yesterday, she became your biggest fan. She's memorized your résumé and can spout forth your sterling accomplishments. I don't know what happened. It's almost as if a switch was thrown in her head, but she'll be delighted to see you."

Emma took Rafe's arm. She'd been churlish enough for one evening.

"Do you think Nina will forgive me?" she asked.

"Of course."

"I suppose she has to. She's church staff."

He laughed. "Not to mention a woman who takes her Christianity seriously."

"I consider what I did hard to forgive."

"It is, but I'm muddling through."

She laughed along with him. If he could forgive her, perhaps she could try to forgive herself.

Emma stopped under a streetlight. "May I have a minute alone, please, to assess the damage to my make-up?" She retrieved the mirror from her purse and studied her face. She cleaned her tear-smudged mascara with a tissue and applied a swipe of lipstick.

She rejoined Rafe, who had moved to the other side of the lamppost. "How do I look?"

"Lovely." He offered his arm again. "Can I ask you a moderately personal question?"

"I suppose."

"Why did you choose to move to Glory?"

"That's a question I get all the time. I came here because I got tired of the rat race in Seattle and felt ready to be my own boss." *No, that's not the real reason. Rafe deserves the truth.* "I also wanted to be as far away from my ex's family as geography allows. They blamed me for his infidelity and made my life unbearable. So I fled. I guess you could say that I let them run me out of Seattle."

"I'll say nothing of the sort. I think you needed a fresh start among nicer people."

Emma nodded. "True, but I wonder how many of those 'nicer people' wish I'd never heard of Glory. This evening was not my finest moment."

"Everything you did at the church will be forgotten in—*oh*, thirty or forty years, tops."

She giggled. "Good! Because I'm not running away again. I've sunk all my capital, financial and emotional, in The Scottish Captain. Here I stay. I cannot do otherwise."

"I'm glad that you intend to stay in Glory," he said in a slightly throaty tone Emma had not heard before.

Probably the chill night air.

Emma noted they'd reached Front Street. The breeze sweeping in from Albemarle Sound felt much cooler. Her red coat looked good, but its thin lining better suited autumn than winter.

"Let's walk faster. I'm beginning to freeze."

"Maybe a kiss will warm you up." Rafe pulled her toward him and gently placed his lips on hers.

Emma was surprised, but not surprised enough to pull away. She tried to analyze the situation, but nothing registered in her brain other than the notion that she should kiss him back.

Silly! I'm already doing that.

She could feel her heart thudding, but her hands and arms seemed disconnected as they wrapped around him.

Rafe was right. I definitely feel warmer now.

She noted that she hadn't exhaled recently. Sooner or later she would have to bring that fact to Rafe's attention.

Later.

Rafe let her move backward. She swallowed gulps of air.

"You have to remember to breathe."

"I have to remember lots of things."

"Me, too. But Kate assures me it will all come back."

"Doubtless, but don't you think we're too old to smooch outdoors?"

"Nope," he said, with a lopsided grin.

"Oh, well…"

Emma kissed him.

Kate's right, too. It does come back.

Afterward, Rafe said, "I distinctly remember that you said 'smooch.' Where did you find a word like that?"

"It's a perfectly good word."

"Perhaps you're right. Kiss me again."

"Wait a minute. We seem to have left out the beginning part where you declare how you feel about me, and vice versa."

"You're right. I'm a bit rusty doing this kind of thing, and it shows. Kate offered to give me a detailed lecture on current practices, but I refused."

"I suppose we can figure it out ourselves."

"Indeed, we can." He added, "Who should go first?"

"The man, of course."

"Well, in that case—" Rafe began.

A wailing siren pierced the night.

"What's that?" Emma asked.

"The siren in front of the fire station. The trucks are responding to a call." Rafe reached for his cell phone. He spoke his name then muttered several numbers. "Ten-four," he said, grimly.

Emma said, "You don't look happy."

"My car is one hundred feet ahead. It'll be faster than walking. Someone just called in a fire at The Scottish Captain."

Rafe parked the Corvette across the street from Glory's two pumpers that were standing in front of The Scottish Captain. He could see two volunteer firemen chatting near the first truck. He read their lack of activity as a good sign that meant the fire had been small, or even a false alarm.

Emma didn't seem to notice the men. She threw open her door even before he'd set the parking brake. Rafe killed the ignition and went after her. He caught up with Emma behind the building, talking with Howard Winston, Glory's fire chief.

"How bad is it?" Emma half said, half shouted. She was doing her best, Rafe could see, to control her perfectly understandable panic.

"Relax, Ms. McCall," the fire chief said gently. He stood a full head taller than Emma and looked twice her size in his bunker coat and helmet. "You had a small fire, but it's out. Look around. No flames. No smoke. Just the smell of singed paint. I'd estimate the damage to be less than three hundred dollars."

"Thank God," Emma said.

"What happened?" Rafe asked.

"A clever case of arson. Someone placed an incendiary device against the back door. It worked as planned, and set the door on fire. Fortunately for you, Ms. McCall, your handyman was working in the garden shed. Hancock called 911 and then put most of the fire out with a garden hose." Howard pointed across the backyard. Hancock Jeffers stood next to a small, squat, clapboard shed speaking with a fireman. "He saved your building, no doubt about it."

"I have to thank him," Emma said. She sprinted across the yard, deftly leaping over the two fire hoses that snaked across the ground.

"Did you question Jeffers yet?" Rafe asked the fire chief.

He tipped his head toward Hancock. "The initial interview going on right now will be the first of many."

"I don't like fortuitous coincidences."

"Me, neither. It was mighty convenient for him to be in the shed at just the right time to extinguish the fire. Our arson investigators will spend some quality time with Mr. Jeffers."

"Show me the firebomb."

"We left it where we found it, positioned against the door. I've never seen anything quite like it."

Rafe followed the fire chief to the Captain's back door. The chief used a compact flashlight to illuminate the back door. Most of the paint had burned off leaving charred wood. Three of the door's four glass panels were broken.

"It's a supersimple firebomb, nothing more than a cardboard wine box filled with pure, two-hundred proof alcohol. The fuse was a lit cigarette stuck into a hole in the top of the box."

Rafe understood immediately. "The cigarette burned down and ignited the highly flammable alcohol."

"The top of the box burned away quickly. The net result was a sheet of flame against the wooden back door. Once the door was fully engaged, the fire would have spread into the kitchen and probably to the rest of the building. These old houses burn like piles of tinder."

Rafe trembled. What if the fire had spread as it was supposed to and Emma had been up in her third-floor owner's apartment?

No! Think about something else.

"But Jeffers was able to put out the fire before it reached the interior," Rafe said.

"He claims that he heard a loud *whooshing* sound and looked out the door of the shed. That's when he saw the flames. He used his cell phone to call us and then turned a garden hose on the fire. Burning alcohol is easy to extinguish with water."

"I wonder why the arsonist didn't use gasoline or paint thinner?" Rafe said.

"Alcohol is a clean-burning accelerant. If the fire had gone all the way, we might never have found the remains of the gadget that started the blaze."

"The glass panels in the doors are broken. Did the fire do that?"

"The fire didn't burn long enough to crack glass. I assume that the arsonist smashed the panels, probably to let the flames inside the house faster."

Rafe nodded. The Scottish Captain had enjoyed divine providence this evening.

"Well, it looks like everything's under control," the

fire chief said. "I'll release the units to return to the firehouse."

"Do you mind if I talk to Jeffers?" Rafe asked.

"Be my guest. Let me know if you learn anything relevant."

Rafe walked toward the garden shed. Emma and Hancock were speaking animatedly, standing in the yellowish light streaming through the open shed door. The fireman who'd interviewed Hancock had left.

"Good evening, Hancock," Rafe said.

"Good evening, sir."

"I'm curious. How did you happen to be in the shed tonight?"

"I already explained to Ms. McCall, sir, but I'll be happy to begin again. This is a week when we planned to do lots of maintenance at the Captain. I'd planned to plant bulbs in the front bed today, but it took me longer than I thought it would to refinish the sink stand in the bathroom. I thought I'd catch up tonight, so I'd be back on schedule tomorrow. With all those lights shining on the front of the Captain, I knew it would be easy to plant the tulips and daffodils tonight."

Rafe glanced at Emma. She seemed to believe Hancock, even though his story didn't make much sense.

"What time this evening did you get here, Hancock?"

"I don't rightly know, Deputy Chief Neilson." He shrugged. "Maybe an hour ago."

"An hour. That's interesting. How many bulbs did you plant so far?"

"Well, in truth, sir, I haven't planted any yet. I've been getting ready."

"A whole hour getting ready—what kind of preparations do you have to do to plant tulip and daffodil bulbs?"

Rafe noted that Hancock had begun to wring his hands, a clear sign of discomfort and increasing nervousness.

Hancock spoke to Emma. "I know that I should've told you what I was doing, Ms. McCall, but I figured I'd be able to do that when you got home from church."

Emma patted his arm. "You have my permission to come and go as you like, Hancock."

His lined face softened with a smile. "Yes, ma'am."

"Did you see anyone else in the backyard?" Rafe asked.

"Not a soul, sir."

"That's odd. I can see the worktable in the shed from here, because it's close to the door. When you were working at the table, you should have had a pretty good view of the yard."

"I don't know about that, sir."

"And do you know what else strikes me as strange?"

"What, sir?"

"If you were working in the shed, you would have had the light on, as it is now. Anyone coming into the yard, an arsonist, for example, would have seen you immediately. I doubt that he or she would have taken the risk of planting a fire starter at the back door with you only a few yards away."

Hancock stared at the ground. "No, sir," he said, softly.

Emma tugged on Rafe's sleeve. "I'm noticeably muzzy-brained tonight because of the shock," she said, "but I finally figured out the purpose of all your questions. You seem to think that Hancock set the fire. That's both impossible and ridiculous! Hancock Jeffers has taken care of this building since before you were born. It's just as much his livelihood as mine. No way he would he burn it down."

Rafe spoke to Hancock. "Ms. McCall is in your

corner. I might be, too, if you told us both the truth about this evening. You weren't working in the shed preparing to plant bulbs, were you?"

Hancock sighed deeply. "No sir. I was asleep in a chair. I didn't mean to fall asleep, but it was dark and cold, and I had wrapped a blanket around myself."

"What woke you up?"

"A funny noise. I think it was glass breaking. I opened the shed door and looked into the backyard. I didn't see anything for about a minute, and then *whoosh,* the Captain's back door was on fire."

Rafe peered into Hancock's face. He seemed to be telling the truth. His new story, at least, didn't sound absurd. Moreover, it fit Howard Winston's theory that the arsonist broke the glass panels in the back door.

Emma moved closer to Hancock. "What were you doing in the shed before you fell asleep?" she asked.

He sighed again. "I've looked after the Captain for the past several nights, ma'am."

"From the shed?"

He nodded. "I've been worried ever since the afternoon that Ms. Kirk visited us. When she died the same day—well, I became even more worried. I knew that something wasn't right. I didn't want anything bad to happen to the Captain." He looked at Emma guiltily. "I hope I didn't do anything wrong."

Emma hugged Hancock. "You did everything right, Hancock," she said. "You're magnificent."

Rafe shook Hancock's hand. "I agree with Ms. McCall, although you did make one mistake tonight. You shouldn't have lied to the fire department."

"No, sir." He stared at the ground again. "I suppose I should find Mr. Winston and tell him the truth."

"An excellent idea," Rafe said, "but before you do, see if you can rustle up a piece of plywood to nail over the broken panels in the door."

"Yes, sir."

Rafe watched Hancock Jeffers go off to the shed, then he took a firm hold of Emma's hand. She smiled at him. "Hadn't you better get home? Kate will be wondering what's become of you."

"I will, when I'm certain you're safe inside with all the doors and windows locked."

Emma read his thoughts. "You think this happened because of my *performance* at church tonight?"

"The arson attempt proves two things. First, we can be fairly certain that the killer was in that choir practice room tonight listening to you. Second, Lily managed to hide those valuable objects in the Captain's secret money safe."

"But why start a fire that might have destroyed everything, including the valuable objects?"

"Because the killer must have decided to destroy them. The objects are probably incriminating. They point to the killer's identity."

"That means that the killer will try again—and again."

Rafe put his arms around Emma. "You're in no danger tonight. I'll assign one of our officers to spend the night in your driveway. Tomorrow morning, first thing, you and I are going to locate the money safe."

"And then?"

"We'll identify the killer, and Glory will be back to normal."

"You make it sound so easy." She added, "Thank you."

"Lock up the building and go to bed. I'll call you in the morning."

"Yes, sir."

"One more thing…" He looked into her eyes. "When we were so rudely interrupted during our walk, I was about to say, I'm falling in love with you, Emma McCall."

"You are?"

"Utterly. Now it's your turn. Even though you're currently muzzy-brained."

"I'm *always* muzzy-brained." Emma put her arms around Rafe. "I think I love you, too, Rafe Neilson."

He kissed her slowly and with an intensity that erased the last of Emma's reservations. She now had no doubts that Rafe loved her and she loved Rafe.

Rafe leaned against the fender of his Corvette and phoned the police dispatcher. "It'll take about a half hour to get someone to Broad Street," she said, after he made his request

"Ten-four."

Rafe zipped up his duty jacket and turned up the collar. He'd stay put until the other officer arrived. He glanced at Emma's bedroom window on the third floor. A moment later, the light near the window went out.

Sleep well, Emma.

"Howdy, Rafe," a voice called from down the block. "I guess all the excitement is over."

"I am *not* in a mood to talk to Rex Grainger," Rafe muttered quietly.

Rafe changed positions on the fender and said, "Hello, Rex. You're about twenty minutes late. The fire engines have left."

"Pity, but at least I'm here in time to get some of the details. Was anyone hurt?"

"No one's hurt. It was a minor blaze—the Captain's back door caught fire."

"Really? A case of spontaneous combustion, I suppose?"

Rafe thought about it. There was no point in not telling Rex. All he had to do to learn the whole story was visit the fire station and talk to Howard. Like it or not, by morning everyone in Glory would know about the arson attempt.

"The fire was started by a homemade incendiary."

"'Homemade incendiary' is too vague a description. I need details."

"You know that I can't give you any specifics yet. The police department and fire department have launched a joint investigation. We intend to find and prosecute the arsonist." He poked the plastic-encased press credential that hung on a lanyard around Grainger's neck. "You can quote me on that."

"Do you think that the Phantom Avenger was responsible?"

Rafe held up fingers to make the point. "One, there is nothing funny about a firebomb. Two, we didn't find a note. Three, the Phantom Avenger pulled his last practical joke a week ago. In other words, the answer is a big *NO*."

"So what happened? Why did the arson attempt fail? The Captain is still here."

"Fortunately, Hancock Jeffers worked late tonight. He put out the fire and called the fire department. The back door is scorched, but that's about it."

Rex looked over at the Captain. "Think she's up to talking?"

Rafe shook his head. "She went to bed—said she felt muzzy-brained."

"I can imagine."

"I'll tell you what she told me, if that would be useful for your story."

Rafe bit back a laugh as Rex yanked a notebook out of his coat pocket at breathtaking speed. "Shoot," the editor said.

"I appreciate the fast response of the Glory Fire Department, but I want to extend a special thank-you to Mr. Hancock Jeffers, whose quick thinking was responsible for minimizing the damage to The Scottish Captain."

"She said that? In those words?"

"Syllable for syllable."

"Sounds kinda formal to me, but you never know."

"You never do," Rafe agreed.

Rafe watched Rex Grainger walk back to his car then drive away. Once again he glanced up at Emma's dark window on the third floor. He meant what he'd said to her. They would locate the secret compartment together, and he would arrest the phony Phantom Avenger.

Life in Glory would return to normal.

And he would start a new life with Emma.

FIFTEEN

"Good morning, my sweet. The good news is that we'll spend the day together. The bad news is that you're on the front page of the *Glory Gazette*."

Emma held the phone to her ear as she looked at her clock through sleep-filled eyes. Six o'clock.

"You told me you'd be here 'first thing' in the morning," she said. "You didn't say you planned to call in the middle of the night."

"You're up earlier than this every day," Rafe said.

"Not when I don't have guests."

"Oh. Then you won't be serving a fabulous breakfast at seven?"

"So that's what this call is all about..." Emma raised her head. Her bedroom felt cold. She pulled her down-filled duvet up to her neck. "Tell you what—you get here at seven and you can help me serve a *reasonably* fabulous breakfast."

"Done!"

"Wait a minute! You said something about the front page of the *Glory Gazette*."

She heard him hesitate. "The fire at the Captain is the lead story."

"I didn't see any media people last night."

"Rex Grainger buttonholed me outside the Captain after you went to bed. He was wearing his reporter's hat."

Emma felt her heart beat faster. "How did he learn about the fire?"

"Well, he lives across the street from the fire department. I'm sure he heard the sirens, and he probably has a police scanner operating 24-7."

"Ugh!" Emma groaned.

"I was very circumspect. I put only the dullest of words in your mouth, in the hope that he would decide not to use them. In fact, he quoted you verbatim."

"Really? What did I say?"

She listened while Rafe read the short article that described "the failed attempt to set fire to one of Glory's architectural gems, the famed Scottish Captain." He added, "Shall I bring you a copy?"

"No need. Mine awaits me outside."

She showered and dressed quickly, choosing an old pair of blue jeans and faded green sweatshirt with the words Glory—A Wee Bit O' Scotland embroidered across the front. Both were ornamented with spots of paint and caulking. If she was going to spend the day on her hands and knees, she might as well wear appropriate clothing.

Emma felt a palpable sadness as she walked downstairs. There was something not right about an empty B and B. Her footfalls on the wooden stair steps seemed to echo throughout the vacant bedrooms. This, she reminded herself, is what the Captain would sound like every morning if tourists should conclude that Glory was too dangerous a town to visit. When would the barrage of unpleasant events finally stop? As if multiple pranks and a murder weren't bad enough, poor little Glory now had an attempted arson to explain.

She made her way to the kitchen and looked around. The only visible signs of damage inside the Captain were shards of glass on the floor near the door. She swept them up and carefully packaged them in paper bags before she put them in the trash can.

She brewed enough fresh coffee to fill a large thermal carafe. They would want to refill their mugs throughout the day, and retrieved two oversize blueberry muffins and a breakfast quiche from the freezer. Because Calvin Constable made extras of most items that could be frozen, the Captain had a good supply of fast breakfasts she could use on days like this.

Her telephone rang again. She looked at the caller ID panel. Glory Community Church. Daniel Hartman must have seen the *Glory Gazette* and wanted to offer his condolences.

Sorry, Pastor, I'm not in the mood to relive last night quite yet.

She unlocked the back door and stepped outside in the early dawn light and chill to inspect the exterior damage. The brief fire had engulfed the lower half of the door and doorway. The decorative millwork was damaged and the paint burned away. The door's upper areas were badly blistered. You didn't have to be an arson expert to realize that if the fire had burned a few seconds more, it would have penetrated the door and reached inside the building.

God bless Hancock Jeffers for caring.

"The Captain will have a new back door," she murmured aloud, "even if I have to pay for it myself." She made a mental note to call her building contractor in Elizabeth City and her insurance agent in Glory.

Emma walked to the front of The Scottish Captain and retrieved her copy of the *Glory Gazette* from the red plastic newspaper box beneath her mailbox. Tempted as she was to look at the front page, she didn't unfold it. Some things were better done indoors, where her neighbors on Broad Street couldn't see her reaction.

Back inside the kitchen, she studied the front page. Beneath the bold headline Arsonist Attacks The Scottish Captain was a photograph of the B and B from her current marketing brochure. The photo had been taken the previous May when all the shrubs and plants looked lush and green. The Scottish Captain looked lovely and inviting.

Perhaps there really is no such thing as bad publicity.

Emma had almost completed the *Gazette*'s crossword puzzle when Rafe knocked on the back door and cautiously pushed it open.

"Good morning," she said.

"Puh-lease! That's a mere salutation. I get to kiss you hello this morning."

Afterward, he said, "I have a present for you."

"Another one?" she replied breathlessly.

Rafe held up an object made of green-and-yellow plastic that reminded Emma of an old-fashioned, jumbo-sized cell phone.

"I called Larry Borstahl this morning," he said, "and had him open Glory Hardware just for me."

"Because you wanted to buy…"

"It's an electronic stud finder—the modern way to locate the studs that support the walls when you want to hang a shelf or a heavy mirror. But it will also track down hidden compartments filled with stuff that's not supposed to be inside a wall." He added, "Instead of tapping the wall, we'll use this gadget."

"You're assuming the money safe is behind a wall. It could be anywhere—floor, ceiling, walls...."

He touched his index finger to her lips. "Have a heart! I can't handle negativity before breakfast."

"You squeeze the orange juice. I'll warm the muffins and the quiche."

"Did you say *quiche?*"

"Calvin Constable makes great quiche. You'll love it."

Twenty minutes into breakfast, Emma said, "If you were a secret compartment, where would you hide?"

Rafe, who had taken a third wedge of quiche, replied, "Before we get to the questions, why don't you summarize everything we know about the Captain's secret compartment?"

"That will take about ten seconds," she said. "The money safe is on the first floor. We know that because the upper two floors have been renovated. The money safe is large enough to hold the contents of two large safe-deposit boxes. We've guessed that, because Lily came here after she tried to rent two such boxes at Glory National Bank. Finally, the money safe is somewhere in the front parlor. We've assumed that, because Lily insisted that Hancock Jeffers let her wait in the parlor."

Rafe put his dish in the sink, then switched on the stud finder. "I'll take the high road—the walls in the parlor. You take the low road—the baseboards and the floor.

Emma and Rafe moved slowly and deliberately around the room, shifting furniture as necessary, lifting area rugs as required, removing pictures and wall hangings as needed.

"Well, that was a fun two hours," he said. "I'm done."

"Me, too," She straightened up and discovered her back ached.

"Now what?"

"I have an idea." Emma thought about asking Rafe to massage her lower back but decided against it. "Let's ask Sara Knoll to help. After all, she's the local guru on secret compartments. She even wrote a few magazine articles on the subject."

"Hmm. I like it. But we can't tell her why we're looking for the money safe. We'll need an alternative explanation."

"In other words, the truth without the details we still have to keep secret."

"Correct."

"Why not tell her I've signed on to the idea of having tourists look for the Captain's secret compartment. That's perfectly true."

Sara arrived fifteen minutes later and explained, "In every house in Glory, each secret compartment is unique. But there are a few things they have in common. Most of the money safes are conveniently located so that they're easy to use."

"Conveniently located, but hard to find," Rafe said.

"Congratulations!" She winked at Rafe. "Hard-to-find is another common characteristic."

"Keep going."

"Well, no tools are needed to open them, just fingers. And don't begin to imagine the fancy motorized panels you see in Hollywood movies. Your money safe will be simple, maintenance-free and clever. You'll say, 'Why didn't I think of that sooner?' when you locate it. Your guests will enjoy the hunt."

"I certainly hope so, but as I told you when I called—" Emma glanced furtively at Rafe "—I don't want my guests moving furniture, lifting floorboards and pounding on my plaster walls. I hoped it would be easier to find."

"How big is the typical secret compartment?"

Sara shrugged. "No one can answer that question. Some compartments were big, some were small. It's all a question of functionality and specifically what the owner wanted to protect. You don't require lots of space to store money, but a wealthy matron who wants to stash a jewel box or two needs a much larger secret compartment." She turned to Emma. "I'd guess that the Captain's money safe is larger than most, because it was designed to serve several residents in the building.

"By the way," Sara continued, "the first place I'd search is your office. If I remember right, your office is connected to this parlor." She added, with a smile, "I took the tour a few years ago."

Emma glanced at Rafe. "Why didn't we think of that? This building was designed as a commercial residence. Where better to hide the money safe than the office?"

Emma tugged the handle; the pocket door slid out of sight into the wall.

"A pocket door!" Sara said merrily. "I haven't seen one of those in years. Do you keep your office locked?"

Emma shook her head. "Most people don't even realize the room is here," she said. "The wallpaper is great camouflage. Besides, all a thief would find inside are reservation slips, bills, receipts and my old computer."

Rafe peered inside the office, then said, "Ladies,

there's only room in this office for one searcher at a time. I'll do it. You two find something else to do."

"How about a cup of coffee?" Emma asked Sara.

"I'd love one," Sara said.

Emma led Sara into the kitchen.

"Now that Rafe can't hear us, I have to ask—how did you manage to talk Rafe into helping you search the Captain?"

Emma felt her face go red.

Oh, my! We forgot to come up with an explanation for Rafe's presence.

Sara laughed. "Your deer-in-the-headlights expression tells me that the gossip I've heard is true."

"What gossip?"

"The word around town is that the two of you were seen on Front Street engaging in some 'friendly' conversation right after the fight at choir practice."

"Well…"

Sara gave Emma a hearty hug. "All I can say is *you go, girl!* You've done what half the women in Glory want to do."

"How do you take your coffee?" Emma asked.

"No, no, no, no, no. We are not going to talk about coffee. I expect to hear the details of your triumph. I want the nitty-gritty details. How did you go about landing the hunk?" She offered a tongue-in-cheek grin. "Who knows? I might be able to apply your expert advice."

When Emma returned to the parlor with Sara close behind, she found Rafe sitting on the floor, looking dejected.

"I lifted the rugs in the office," he said. "I probed each floorboard, and I ran the stud locator over every inch of wall surface. There's no secret compartment.

"I wonder…" Sara surveyed the front parlor, her face becoming less happy with each passing second. "I'm beginning to have a bad feeling about The Scottish Captain." She used her knuckles to tap the wall next to a light switch. "Most of the old buildings in Glory were partially renovated during the 1920s to install proper electrical wiring. I'll bet your money safe was destroyed back then. That would explain why no one's ever been able to find the silly thing."

Rafe nodded. "You could be right. We certainly don't seem to be making any progress."

Emma added her own nod. "I seem to have invited you along on a wild-goose chase, Sara. I apologize."

"You invited me here to play the expert—one of my favorite activities. I love giving lectures. In fact, I should apologize to you for bending your ear, but of course I won't." She laughed. "Are you coming this evening?"

Emma felt bewildered by Sara's question. "This evening?"

"Check your messages. Daniel called an emergency meeting of the choir at seven o'clock." Her gaze shifted from Emma to Rafe. "Daniel expects every singer to attend."

Emma remembered the phone call from the church that she had ignored.

"I'll be there," she said.

"So will I," Rafe said.

"In that event, my work here is done." Sara hugged them both and left.

"Do you think Sara is right about the money safe?" Emma said. "After all, she's an expert."

Rafe shook his head. "Lily Kirk was the expert. Sara is an interested journalist, at best. She's guessing, although I did like her notion that the money safe is somewhere in the office."

Emma brushed carpet lint off her jeans. "'Once more into the breach.'"

The stupid money safe had to be somewhere.

"I'll do the office again," Rafe said. "Maybe I've missed something."

"Okay," Emma nodded. "I'll repeat my futile search of the parlor."

Rafe recalibrated the stud finder—just in case—and pressed it against the wall, just as his cell phone rang.

He unclipped the phone from his belt and looked at the screen. *Chief Porter Mobile Phone.*

This won't be a cheerful conversation.

He slid the pocket door shut. There was no need for Emma to hear him get chewed out.

"What can I do for you, Chief?" Rafe said.

"Oh, I just wanted to verify that you're still working for us. It's been a while since you visited Police Headquarters."

"I'm at The Scottish Captain looking for a key piece of evidence pertaining to the death of Lily Kirk."

"I hope you find it, Rafe." He paused. "I can't keep the lid on this any longer. We need to make an arrest. My inclination is to pull in the high school kids responsible for the pranks. We can interview the lot of them and see what develops."

"You know they had nothing to do with Lily's death."

"No, Rafe. I don't know that. Not for a fact."

"Give us two more days, Chief. Emma McCall and I are making real progress. I'm sure we'll have something for you by then."

"I don't have forty-eight more hours to invest in a guess and a hope. You've got until noon tomorrow. That's the best I can do."

The line went dead. Rafe tried to return the cell phone to his belt, but the clip didn't engage and the phone fell to the floor. When he dropped to his knees to retrieve it, his gaze fell on the rear side of the sliding pocket door. The lower half of the door had a different texture than the upper half. Moreover, there were four round decorative knobs—one at each corner of the lower wooden panel.

He opened the door halfway. "Emma! I may have found it."

She squeezed into the office and knelt down beside him.

He slid the door shut and said, "Take a look."

"I see it! The bottom panel definitely looks different than the top."

He ran the stud locator over the panel and studied its indicator lights. "There's something behind the panel— it's not air and it's not wood."

Emma grinned at him. "Do you think those knobs turn?"

Rafe gently rotated the knobs counterclockwise. The lower wooden panel began to lift away from the door. A moment later, the panel fell loose against his knees.

"Books!" Emma said. "The compartment is full of books stacked on their edges."

Rafe lifted the closest book, a substantial volume bound in blue cloth, and examined it: *Moby-Dick; or, The Whale,* by Herman Melville. Rafe opened the cover and found a bookplate handwritten in brown ink: "'This book belongs to Samuel Caruthers, July, 1865.'" He turned another page: Harper & Brothers, 1851. First American Edition.

"I think this is a first edition of Moby-Dick," he said. "In great condition."

"You're going to tell me it's worth thousands of dollars."

"*Tens* of thousands. Maybe a hundred thousand. There aren't many copies in circulation. A warehouse fire destroyed most of the first edition before it could be sold."

"Yikes!" She reached into the compartment and brought out a volume with a tan cloth cover. Rafe looked over her shoulder.

Red Badge of Courage by Stephen Crane. "'From the Library of Jacob Caruthers, May, 1895.'"

"The date on the bookplate is the same year the book was published. Do you think it's another first edition?

"Probably."

"Worth a fortune?"

"Many of the theft cases I worked on Long Island involved first editions. If I remember right, this book is worth less than Moby-Dick."

"But still a lot?"

"About half of what I'll earn this year." He pointed toward the corner of the compartment. "Get me the volume that's covered in green cloth. I've seen that kind of binding before."

"Aha," Emma said, "*The Adventures of Huckleberry Finn* by Mark Twain."

Rafe opened the cover: "'This book belongs to Samuel Caruthers, February, 1885.'"

"Another first edition?" she said.

"Definitely." He looked at the compartment from a few different angles. "I count a total of seventeen books.

If they're all nineteenth-century first editions in fine condition, I'll bet the total value is more than a half million dollars."

"A nifty motive for murder."

"And for theft. I'm fairly sure the theft came first."

"Lily…" Emma said softly.

"It's not hard to figure out what happened. Lily found them among the 'junk books' from John Caruthers's attic, and she recognized how valuable they were. No one else knew they existed, so why not keep them?" He took Emma's hand. "But Lily made a fatal mistake. She decided that she needed help, so she told someone else."

"What kind of help would she need? She already had the books in her possession."

"How do you convert a rare book into cash when you don't have a provenance that proves you're the legitimate owner?"

"Well, *I suppose*… Okay, first thing I would do…"

"My point exactly. You don't know, and neither did Lily."

"But Sam Lange probably does know."

Rafe nodded. "I'd guess that Sam has a crooked acquaintance or two in the used-book trade." He let himself sigh. "He's our prime suspect. He killed Lily."

"For what purpose? Why would Sam kill Lily?"

"I can think of lots of reasons. Maybe Sam wanted all of the money for himself? Maybe he got wind that Lily was trying to cheat him? Maybe they just got on each other's nerves? Whoever coined the old maxim is wrong—there isn't much honor among thieves."

"But Sam is so…*nice*."

"And your point is? Look how it fits. Sam provided the book of practical jokes to the original Phantom

Avenger. Sam had clearly worked out a bizarre plan to kill Lily."

Rafe put his arm around Emma. "I don't know of a more grim aspect of police work than arresting a friend, but it has to be done."

"I know it does." Emma brushed a tear from her eyes. "What are we going to do with these books?"

"We'll leave them right where they are. The Captain's secret compartment is probably the safest place in Glory."

SIXTEEN

Standing in the back of the sanctuary, Rafe waved his hand as Daniel spoke. "One… Two… Three…" into the microphone up front.

"You sound fine, Padre," Rafe said. He'd arrived at church at six forty-five in the hope that Sam Lange would also show up at the meeting early.

"Since our sound system seems to be working, I'll offer a prayer before the rest of the choir arrives." Daniel cleared his throat; Rafe bowed his head. "Heavenly Father," Daniel began, "we are Your Son's church, and we fail Him miserably when we fight with one another. You alone know the outcome of tonight's meeting—whether we'll end the turmoil that threatens Glory Community Church or continue down the path to destruction. I ask Your Holy Spirit to be with us this evening, to help us cope and, if it be Your will, to heal the breach that has divided us. In Jesus's name we pray."

Rafe moved closer to the pastor. "Daniel, you suddenly look a bit green around the gills."

Daniel nodded, then sighed. "I don't feel too swift this evening. In fact, I just murmured another prayer that if it's necessary for me to throw up tonight, please let it be after the meeting." He brought a roll of antacids out of his shirt pocket and popped one in his mouth. "The fact is, I'm worried. What happens here tonight will save this church—and my pastorate—or else complete the destruction of Glory Community and send me off to an early retirement of fishing and writing." He managed a sour smile. "Maybe I'm ready for that."

Rafe felt his own stomach muscles tighten. Daniel was right. Glory Community was in great danger. Many another healthy congregations had been destroyed for equally nonsensical reasons. Rafe wondered if even a letter from the Apostle Paul could reverse the split.

He followed Daniel to the side of the sanctuary to help two volunteers from the hospitality committee set up a refreshment table of cookies and pink lemonade. Daniel had obviously waived the usual rule that no food or drink could be brought into the sanctuary other than the bread and the wine for the Lord's Supper. And why not? A few stains on the carpet wouldn't mean much if the choir split in two and the congregation followed its lead.

Rafe poured himself a glass of lemonade and acknowledged the various hellos he received from other members of the choir as they dribbled in.

When he looked back at Daniel, the pastor was chatting in the center aisle with a highly animated Sara Knoll. "I can't take much more of this," she said, loudly enough for Rafe to hear. "I'm seriously thinking of leaving."

"Leaving? You mean leave the church?"

Sara nodded, a steely glint in her eyes. "Maybe even Glory, too. This whole fight is *atrocious*. My committee has screeched to a halt. We are hopelessly deadlocked. All we can agree on is that we will never be able to reach an agreement. Sane adults don't act this way."

Rafe sipped lemonade and managed to filter Daniel's reply out of the general din. "I know this has been hard on you, Sara, but I'd hate to see you leave Glory or the church. All I can say is that with God's help we'll get past this bump in the road."

Rafe felt a poke in his ribs. "So it's true," Emma said. "Small-town cops eavesdrop on other people's conversations."

Rafe reached for her hand; she pushed it away. "Uh-uh," she continued. "People are already talking about us."

"What are they saying?"

"That we have a blossoming relationship."

"And your point is?"

"Let's change the subject. This meeting is not about us." She leaned closer to Rafe. "I haven't seen Sam, have you? It looks like the other choir members have arrived."

"Nope. Sam's not here yet, and I don't know why."

"Apparently neither does Nina McEwen."

Rafe turned around. The members of the choir appeared to have learned nothing from Daniel's previous lecture. Once again, the dysfunctional group of singers had arranged themselves according to their traditionalist, contemporary, or independent affiliation. Nina was counting noses and had stopped among the Contemporaries.

"Has anyone seen Sam Lange this evening?" Nina said.

Sara Knoll waved her hand and answered before any of the singers did. "I was in Sam's bookstore this afternoon, Nina. He told me that he planned to attend a used-book fair going on in Hampton, Virginia. He said that he'd try to get back to Glory as early as he could, but it would probably be after the meeting started."

Rafe whistled softly to himself and made a snap decision. He would have to share his plans with Daniel.

"Daniel, may I have two minutes of your time? I have something important to discuss with you."

Sara rolled her eyes. "I *hate* being left out of boy talk."

Emma touched Sara's arm. "This time, the girls have something to talk about, too. We found the *you-know-what* after you left The Scottish Captain."

Sara gasped. She held up her lemonade glass and managed to croak, "The lemonade went down the wrong way."

Rafe peered at Daniel, who wasn't smiling. "Is a private chat essential?" he asked. "I was just about to begin the meeting."

Rafe donned his most serious expression. "I need to talk to you now, Pastor."

"Okay. We'll have some privacy in the front of the sanctuary." Before he finished speaking, Rafe found himself trotting after Daniel down the center aisle.

Daniel turned and said, "Now, what's this all about?"

"If you were to look outside the church, you'd see two uniformed police officers standing in the shadows."

"Are you worried about another choir fistfight?"

"Hardly. I'm going to arrest Sam Lange when he arrives."

"Arrest Sam?" Daniel croaked. "For what?"

"I can't say anything more right now, but I wanted you to know."

"I almost wish that you hadn't said anything." Daniel inhaled and exhaled rhythmically, seemingly to relax himself. "I'm hoping to reconcile the choir to-night. The last thing the group needs is a high-stress situation at the end." He added, "Can you at least wait until after the meeting?"

Rafe could feel his countenance soften as he considered the request. He let himself nod. "Okay. We'll try our best to be nondisruptive."

"Thank you, but I give you fair warning. I intend to pray that Sam doesn't get back from Hampton until long after the meeting is finished." He leaned over and gave Rafe a robust hug. "Incidentally, I wish you and Emma McCall the best. I hope you'll ask me to perform the ceremony when the time comes."

Rafe coughed in surprise. Then he saw a sly smile cross Daniel's face. Rafe returned it with one of his own. "I thought that taking revenge on a poor police-man was not a Christian thing to do."

Daniel winked at Rafe then glanced at his watch. "Time to begin."

Rafe moved to join the choir sitting in the pews. He noted that everyone connected to the choir was here except Sam. Sixteen singers. Nina McEwen, looking unhappy. And Sara Knoll, looking puzzled.

When Rafe sat down, Daniel began. "My friends, I'd like to open our meeting with a reading from Philip-pians, specifically verses 4:2-3.

"'I plead with Euodia and I plead with Syntyche to agree with each other in the Lord. Yes, and I ask you, loyal *Syzygus,* to help these women who have con-tended at my side in the cause of the gospel...'

"It's pretty obvious that Paul was trying to stop a messy fight in the church at Philippi. Paul reminded his old friends that we all should agree with one another in the Lord. Christians should do their best to cooperate with other Christians. If they can't, then a third party can be called in to help mend the rift.

"Paul knew that Euodia and Syntyche were decent people who had forgotten that they were supposed to love one another. In the verse that follows, Paul urges them to 'rejoice in the Lord, to stop fighting, and to let their gentleness be evidenced to the whole church.'"

Rafe looked at the choir members around him. Several had lowered their gazes, but a few seemed to be glaring at Daniel.

"Funny, isn't it?" Daniel went on. "As Christians we should all listen to Paul's wonderful advice, but the sinner inside us makes us too stubborn for that. I hear feet shuffling, and I know some of you want to leave. But I beg you not to go."

Daniel took a deep breath. "For the past few weeks, I've been striving to find words to say that will change your minds or your positions. My primary source, of course, was the Bible, but then I thought, why not look for good words in the other area of my life. Specifically, the U.S. Army."

A few heads shot up.

Rafe chuckled. *Well, that got their attention.*

"After all," Daniel went on, "I'm supposed to bring all of my spiritual gifts to the task of pastoring this church—including the gifts I developed earlier in my career."

"Like what?" Richard Squires said.

"Like discernment. I was in the military for a lot of years. I don't consider myself a military strategist, but I came across many strategic principles that impressed me. One of them tells you to make sure that you don't overstate the similarities between the past and the present or ignore the differences between the past and the present…"

"I don't get what you mean," Michelle Porter Engle shouted from her pew.

"Hang on. I'm about to give you a good example."

Rafe sensed a new excitement in the room. Daniel seemed more animated, the choir more responsive.

"What happened at this church when we received John Caruthers's bequest?" Daniel said.

Dave Early raised his hand. "We set up a committee to decide how to spend it."

"Precisely," Daniel said. "We created a committee, just like we always do."

"And…" Becky Taylor said. "Did we do something wrong?"

"Not at all, but we ignored the simple fact that the bequest is very different from any other gift we've ever received."

"In what way is it different?" asked Jacqueline Naismith.

"In every way," Daniel replied. "John Caruthers gave us a bigger gift than we've ever before received." He paused. "It's too much money, way too much money, because the sheer size of the gift encouraged both sides to plan grandiose refinements to the sanctuary. In doing that, we forgot that we have a critical responsibility to support the mission of this church."

Rafe heard murmuring on either side. No surprise. No one had talked about the mission before, other than some vague platitudes about John Caruthers's instruction that the bequest support the church's ministry of music.

Daniel continued, "Here's what I propose. I intend to recommend to the Elders that we give away one-half of the bequest to poorer churches to support their music ministries. Just so you understand what I'm talking about, and for those of you who have trouble with the division of large numbers, that's three hundred thousand dollars."

Someone coughed.

Daniel pressed on. "Giving this money away will honor John Caruthers's wishes far better than if we spend the money ourselves. It will mean that Glory Community has a *true* ministry of music."

Rafe glanced to his left and right. The singers seemed to understand—and agree with—Daniel's suggestion. Many were nodding.

"I also propose," Daniel said, "that we divide the remaining three hundred thousand dollars into three equal sums. The Traditionalists will receive one hundred thousand dollars to spend on a new electronic organ and the Contemporaries will get one hundred thousand dollars to spend on sound systems and projectors and computers."

"But what about the sanctuary, Daniel?" someone called out. "Aren't we going to spend anything on that?"

Daniel shook his head. "No. We leave the sanctuary alone. It looks fine to me just as it is."

"What about the rest of the money?" another said.

"Ah, you folks *can* add. Well, I propose that we spend the remaining one hundred thousand dollars to fund free concerts throughout the region to showcase both our excellent choir and our great contemporary band as part of Glory's outreach and ministry. Wouldn't it be wonderful if we could use your musical talents to bring more folks to Christ?"

Rafe held his breath. Nobody in the pews moved. Nobody said a word. He wondered how this would end.

Then Rebecca Taylor began to clap.

Rafe guessed that Rebecca's response would be contagious. Lane Johnson joined in and so did Candy Cole. A moment later, the entire choir was clapping.

Debbie Akers burst into tears, and Jake Moore offered her his handkerchief. Rafe hugged Emma and looked over her shoulder at Daniel, who seemed relaxed for the first time this evening.

Rafe murmured, "Thank you, God." Daniel's unusual message had a profound effect on the choir. With God's help it would change people's hearts.

Emma delighted in Rafe's touch as he slipped his arm around her shoulders and steered her toward his Corvette. "Daniel's a genius," he said, as he opened the door for her.

"I'm still teary eyed." She climbed in. "Daniel has found a perfect compromise—a terrific way to spend the Caruthers bequest in a way that encourages good stewardship."

"'For where your treasure is, there your heart will be also.'"

"That's one of my favorite verses from the Gospel of Matthew. It was simply wrong to think of spending all that money on this one church. We learned a valuable lesson, no pun intended."

"Speaking of money," he said, "what happened to Sara Knoll? She must be super relieved that the congregational log jam is finally broken."

"I saw her earlier, but I guess she left during Daniel's speech."

"And I guess that Sam Lange never made it back from Hampton, Virginia."

"In a way, I'm glad," Emma said.

"Me, too. That meeting was too amazing to dampen with an arrest." He added, "We'll find him tomorrow. He can't go far, and he won't be a tough nut to crack."

Emma used the quiet time as they drove to The Scottish Captain to think about one of the phrases Daniel had spoken. It seemed only an instant had passed when Rafe parked across the street in front of a full-size pickup truck.

"I've been such a dunce," she said.

He laughed. "About what?"

"I stopped rejoicing in the Lord. Two years ago, when I was miserably unhappy, I decided not to be a member of a church."

"But you still go every Sunday to be part of our choir. And you sing praise to the name of the Lord most high, as the Psalmist wrote."

"It's not the same thing, silly." She turned so that Rafe wouldn't see the tears in her eyes. "I've just realized that God helped me through a rough patch in my life…and that the rough patch itself had a purpose. It was part of His plan to bring me to Glory."

"And to me," Rafe said softly. He put his arm around her shoulder and handed her a tissue.

"Not only did I refuse to rejoice in the Lord, but also I cut myself off from church—and, if I am honest, from God, too."

"You don't sound cut off. What's more, I think I've just heard what I would call quiet rejoicing."

"You think so?"

"Definitely." Rafe leaned across his sports car's gearshift lever and kissed her.

Emma clutched Rafe's arm around her during half

of the short walk to the Captain's front door, then abruptly moved away from him and froze in the middle of the street.

"What's wrong?" Rafe asked.

"I may be loony, but we just saw a pickup truck parked on Broad Street that I've never seen parked here before. Lily told me she was pushed off the road by a pickup truck. And, I distinctly remember turning off the light in the kitchen before we left. The light's on now."

"There's nothing loony about that."

She saw him reach inside his jacket and unsnap the leather loop that secured the small off-duty pistol inside the holster that he wore tucked into the small of his back.

"Does the lock on the back door still work?" he asked. "Can you unlock it from the outside with your key?"

"I haven't tried yet."

"Now's the perfect time."

She followed Rafe footstep for footstep as he slowly made his way along the narrow flagstone path that led to the back door.

"You unlock the door, then stand aside. Don't come in until I tell you to."

To her surprise, she managed to slip the key into the lock on her first try. She turned the key slowly and felt the dead bolt move sideways. The fire had obviously not reached the lock mechanism.

Rafe signaled her to move out of the way. "Wait near the shed," he whispered, "I don't want you in the line of fire if there's any shooting."

"Don't say that!" she whispered back. "You told me that Sam Lange would be an easy nut to crack." She added, "Shouldn't you call for backup?"

"Are you sure you didn't leave the light on earlier, or that you've never seen that pickup truck before?"

"Well…" Her mind felt curiously blank. "When you put it that way, I'm not sure of anything."

"I don't want to call for backup if we're just guessing." He leaned over and kissed her. "Now, stand near the shed."

Rafe held his gun at his side and kicked the bottom of the door. It sprang open. He moved inside the house with the swift grace of a dancer.

Emma couldn't see into the kitchen from where she stood close to the shed.

This is silly!

She moved closer to the open door, peeked around the frame, and saw Rafe walking around the kitchen, wearing an extremely puzzled expression. Sam Lange was sitting at the kitchen table, looking very unhappy, a strip of silver duct tape across his mouth, a bruise on his forehead and his hands secured together with a large nylon cable tie.

A voice behind Emma said, "Rafe, please set your gun down gently on the table and don't make any sudden moves. I'm holding a large caliber automatic. It's pointed at the small of Emma's back."

Emma was surprised to hear intense malice in Sara Knoll's voice. And then Emma felt something hard and cold against her spine.

A gun barrel! Sara does have a gun. And I'm her target.

SEVENTEEN

Rafe followed Sara's instructions and placed his pistol on the kitchen table. He thought about Emma standing behind him with Sara's gun aimed at her back. He needed Emma to stay calm while he tried to sort out the situation.

We're in a mess.

The moment he'd seen the tape on Sam's mouth he realized that he and Emma had made a terrible miscalculation. Pointing the finger at Sam had been too obvious, too easy. Emma had been right; Sam was too nice.

Unlike Sara Knoll.

"Okay, everyone," Sara said. "The first thing we're going to do is to relocate to the front parlor. This kitchen is too cramped. I want all of you at more than arm's length—especially you, Rafe."

"Thank you for caring," Rafe said.

"I've always respected your abilities," Sara said. "It really is a pity I have to do what I have to do."

"I'm not going anywhere," Emma said.

"Come now, Emma," Sara said. "You really don't want me to start shooting before I have to, do you?" She added, "Emma, do something useful. Help Sam to his feet. He's had a rough night. I had to give him an encouraging whack with my pistol to get him to join us. While you're at it, take the duct tape off his mouth."

Rafe smelled Emma's perfume as she walked past him to reach Sam. At last, he could see her. The color had left her cheeks; she looked frightened.

"I'm sorry, Sam," Emma said, her voice cracking. "This is going to hurt." She helped him stand then dislodged the tape in one long pull.

Rafe winced as Sam issued a loud, long *yeow!*

"Everyone is doing fine," Sara said. "We're making progress. I'm proud of you, Rafe. You've resisted the temptation to turn around or engage in any useless heroics."

"You're the one holding the gun."

"Yes I am, Rafe. A big one. A Glock automatic equipped with a seventeen-round magazine."

Rafe looked down at his own Walther PPK automatic on the table. Even if he could reach it, even if he could aim it at Sara quickly enough to get off a shot, the small 9 mm short cartridges in the PPK had limited stopping power. Sara would have more than enough time to get off a half-dozen powerful forty-caliber rounds at them.

Hardly a fair exchange.

He heard Sara walking toward him. She continued around the table until she was facing him. She hadn't lied. The pistol in her hand was a Glock with its safety off. It was pointed directly at Emma.

"Rafe," Sara said. "You help Sam through the swinging door and into the hallway. I'll be right behind you with Emma. Don't be cute with the door. Don't try to swing it at me, or Emma will be toast. Understand?"

"Understood," he answered.

Rafe decided they could do nothing to challenge Sara in the kitchen or hallway. Maybe the situation would improve in the parlor. The important thing, though, was to keep her talking. He helped Sam though the door and continued walking slowly toward the parlor.

"Not so fast, Rafe," Sara said. "I don't want to lose sight of you and neither does Emma." Sara ended with a laugh.

Rafe paused to let Sara and Emma catch up, and then he moved through the doorway into the parlor.

Sara flipped on the light. "Rafe, you stand there on the left side." She pointed to the front of the parlor. "And you, Emma, stand on the right side. Sam, you relax on the sofa. Take a nap if you'd like. I'm going to get comfy back here on this lovely chaise lounge."

Rafe leaned against the wall. So far, Sara hadn't made a single mistake, but what was she trying to accomplish? Did manipulating the three of them have a purpose?

"Lady and gentlemen, I am going to ask nicely, but only once. Where are the seventeen first editions?"

Rafe's back straightened. *Sara doesn't know where the books are.* In an instant, he realized that Emma hadn't told Sara how to find the money safe. Their "girl talk" back at the church hadn't included specifics. That's why she hadn't used her Glock on anyone.

Well done, Emma!

"Why should we tell you?" Emma said. "I've figured out what you plan to do. You are going to kill us and put the blame on Sam."

Rafe saw Sara's eyes sparkle. Emma was right. Sara would make it appear that Sam shot them and then Sara would conveniently kill Sam—claiming it was self-defense. Rafe could imagine the Chief questioning Sara:

"Why did you become Sam's target?"

"Because he knew that I had helped locate the money safe and had seen the collection of first editions."

"What went wrong, Sara?" Rafe said, "We know it was you who made an arrangement with Lily to steal the books. What happened? Did you decide not to give Lily her share?"

She laughed. "No. Lily decided not to give me *my* share. A week ago, she announced that she intended to follow the Caruthers bequest to the letter. The ten most valuable first editions would go to the church. The other seven would go to poor old Sam." She looked at Sam. "Lily felt sorry for you. She hated the idea of giving you those worthless boxes of books each week. She intended to spice up future deliveries with a rare, first edition in each carton."

Sara rose to her feet and pointed her pistol at Emma. "There's been enough chatter, Rafe. Tell me how to find the money safe or your budding romance will be cut short."

Rafe could see Emma glancing at the bookcase near the window. She made small, slow moves toward it. Sara didn't seem to mind. Not with a Glock automatic in her hand.

"You aren't planning to jump out of the window, are you?" Sara said to Emma.

"I don't suppose you'd let me," Emma replied.

What happened next was over in a flash of bronze that Rafe witnessed out of the corner of his eye.

He saw Emma's outstretched arm abruptly swing around like a flywheel.

He heard a stomach-turning crunch—a nasty sound of metal striking bone.

He watched Sara Knoll fold in half silently then crumple to the floor in an insensible heap.

He spotted the Glock pistol go skittering along the wooden floor and come to a stop under the chaise lounge.

Rafe leaped across the room and retrieved the pistol. He looked at Sara; she was unconscious and had an ugly bruise blossoming over her left eye. He felt her carotid artery; there was a reasonably strong pulse. Next to her on the floor was an odd-looking bronze sphere that seemed to have stitching on its newly dented surface.

Rafe moved quickly to Emma's side. He drew her close and kissed her forehead. Her fearful look had given way to a curiously satisfied expression.

"Strike one," she said.

Emma poured a glass of iced tea for Rafe. "It's not my fault that you didn't know I played softball back in Seattle."

"She's right, Dad," Kate said. "I offered to show you the dossier I had prepared, but you were too busy to read it."

The other guests at the Sunday dinner laughed. Rafe threw up his hands in a gesture of defeat. The others laughed even harder.

Emma felt quite proud that she'd been able to organize a sit-down dinner for eight only three days after the arrest of Sara Knoll for the murder of Lily Kirk. Rafe had told Emma that several other charges would follow—as soon as the police tallied up her many crimes and misdemeanors, including:

Attempting to run Lily's old Ford Taurus off State Route 34A

Setting fire to The Scottish Captain's back door

Committing burglary and vandalism at Lily Kirk's town house

Kidnapping Sam Lange

Committing aggravated assault on Emma, Rafe and Sam.

"The list of her crimes goes on and on," Rafe had said a few minutes earlier. "There's not much chance of meeting Sara out of prison for the next seventy or eighty years."

Emma might have cheered had she not noted the somber expression on Daniel's face. She quickly reminded herself that a prayer for Sara Knoll was a more appropriate form of expression for the newest member of Glory Community Church.

Emma was sitting at the head of the large Sunday dinner table that Hancock Jeffers had assembled by pushing three four-person tables together in the dining room that now served as the Captain's breakfast room. Emma had covered the temporary rectangle with a gold tablecloth and had given it a pre-Thanksgiving look by adding a centerpiece that consisted of a raffia cornucopia stuffed with fruit and nuts.

On her right were Nina McEwen, Daniel Hartman and Kate Neilson.

On her left were Sam Lange, Hancock Jeffers and Calvin Constable.

Rafe Neilson sat facing Emma at the other end of the table.

Calvin's seat was more ceremonial than real because

he kept bouncing up to make trips to the Captain's kitchen. He had cooked Sunday dinner and was also serving it.

The look in the dining room was elegant yet informal—also an apt description of Calvin's cooking. He had created a new dish for the occasion: "Scottish Turkey." He planned to make several to include in Thanksgiving baskets that would be distributed to needy families and had decided to test the recipe on his friends.

"Scottish Turkey," he explained proudly, "is stuffed with oat and barley dressing. I created the unique plaid pattern on the turkey's breast with interlocking strips of red, green and yellow peppers."

Emma looked at her tablemates with satisfaction. She knew that the quiet time at the Captain would be over in a few hours. Four guests would arrive later this evening, the first of many who would spend the holidays at The Scottish Captain.

"I've been comparing notes with my associates at the other B and Bs in town," Hancock Jeffers said. "The phone lines are burning up with new reservations."

Emma nodded. "It's quite a mystery. Visitors seem to have suddenly discovered Glory."

"There's nothing mysterious about it," Kate said. "Every newspaper in North Carolina is running stories about Sara Knoll and Glory. We're famous."

"*Infamous,* more like it," Daniel said glumly.

Nina jumped in. "Kate is absolutely right. There's nothing like a juicy murder—particularly one involving a minor celebrity like Sara Knoll—to excite the imagination. Tourists seem to ask themselves, Why not stop in a town that is home to a fascinatingly bizarre crime?"

Sam Lange raised his forefinger and took the floor. "I move that the Glory Chamber of Commerce organize a Sara Knoll walking tour of Glory. Visitors can start with Sara's house on West Osborn Street, move on to Lily Kirk's town house, browse for a while at the Glory Book Nook, take a moment to marvel at the bruise on my forehead and then linger in Sara's favorite pew at Glory Community Church."

"I think we can do without the last item," Daniel said.

Nina patted his hand. "What I hope is that the next woman who moves to Glory will take a fancy to you, Daniel."

"That would be so cool," Kate said, clapping. "After my dad, you are the most awesome man in Glory. I wish I was twenty years older."

"What about me?" Sam asked. "How awesome am I?"

"Well—" Kate hesitated.

Emma took over. "You'll be wildly awesome when you get your hands on the seven first editions you inherited and convert them into cash."

Daniel moaned. "Please don't mention those infernal books. The last thing the church needs is more money, not when we've just agreed on how to spend the first load."

Rafe chuckled. "Sorry, Daniel, but our preliminary estimate gives a market value for the books in excess of five hundred thousand dollars. You may have to deal with another three hundred fifty thousand dollars at the church once they are sold to a book dealer."

This time, Daniel groaned loudly.

Emma took pity on the put-upon pastor and changed the topic of discussion. "What fascinates me about Sara Knoll is how many rotten things she knew how to do."

"Ah," Rafe said, "the North Carolina State Bureau of Investigation has been working overtime to explain Sara's expertise. She apparently learned how to handle a gun, build a firebomb and drive cars off the road during her travels around the world as a journalist. She spent quality time with a long list of unsavory characters and groups."

"I have a question," Sam said. "Sara brought me to The Scottish Captain in a big pickup truck, but she drove around Glory in a Chevy Malibu. What's the story?"

Emma noted Rafe's broad grin. He seemed in his element, telling war stories about police work.

"It turns out," Rafe began, "that Sara owns a second home out west in Black Mountain, North Carolina. She kept the pickup truck there, except when she needed an unfamiliar vehicle in Glory to commit a crime.

"Her other home was really the headquarters for her nefarious dealings. The NCSBI found a carton of ignition noisemakers. She apparently bought them from a supplier of illegal fireworks."

"And don't forget the printers, Dad," Kate said. "The ones she used to forge the notes from the Phantom Avenger."

Rafe nodded. "We even found the files for the two fake notes on her computer."

Emma looked across the table at Rafe and registered her delight at his animation and enthusiasm. She had no doubts that she loved him. Her eyes suddenly locked with his. A pity, she thought, that they were at a dinner table with six other people.

A long kiss would be lovely.

Emma watched with surprise as Rafe pushed back his chair. He circled the table to reach her. He gently took her hand and beckoned her to rise.

What could he be thinking?

"Kiss me," he said softly.

"In front of everyone?" Emma replied. "Including your daughter and our pastor?"

"Absolutely."

He lifted her chin and pressed his lips to hers.

Emma heard a curious roar. It took her a moment to realize that all her guests at the dinner table were cheering.

* * * * *

Watch for Ron & Janet Benrey's next cozy mystery
GONE TO GLORY

On sale in September 2007
from Steeple Hill Love Inspired Suspense.

Dear Reader,

When we wrote *Glory Be!* we imagined Glory, North Carolina, as the friendly sort of small town where neighbors have known each other for years, where local church choirs are filled with interesting characters and where people are not afraid to leave their doors unlocked most of the time. Glory may be fictional, but we know there are many real towns across the nation that offer the innocence we set out to portray in our novel.

Perhaps you live in a town like Glory? Perhaps you want to?

Glory is the kind of place that many people see as a latter-day Garden of Eden, as an escape. Emma McCall sought refuge from a hectic big-city job and a faithless ex-husband. Rafe Neilson wanted to get away from a dangerous metropolis full of grim memories.

Neither succeeded at first, because Glory had a "serpent"—a ruthless killer who transformed the idyllic town into a scary place, until good managed to triumph over evil and restore the balance. That's part of the fun of a cozy mystery: by the end of the story "God's in his heaven. All's right with the world!" to quote the well-known line by Robert Browning.

We hope you enjoyed your first visit to Glory. Watch for more romantic cozy mysteries starring some of the friends you made in *Glory Be!*

Janet Benrey

Ron Benrey

QUESTIONS FOR DISCUSSION

1. Both Rafe and Emma tried to flee sad memories and start new lives in Glory. Emma hoped to put a broken marriage behind her; Rafe wanted to escape a disaster that caused his wife's death. Did they succeed? Why or why not?

2. Have you ever tried to start over in some aspect of your life? What lessons did you learn when you did? What role did faith play in your efforts?

3. Christians are told to love one another and not engage in the kind of strife that went on at Glory Community Church. What do you think was the chief cause of the conflict between the Traditionals and the Contemporaries?

4. Rafe's daughter, Kate, abruptly challenged Emma's authority. Why do you think she behaved the way she did? What eventually changed her mind?

5. Practical jokes of the sort carried on in *Glory Be!* may not seem funny to their victims. What should the Christian perspective be toward practical joking?

6. The apostle Paul warned that "the love of money is a root of all kinds of evil," 1 Timothy 6:10. What different kinds of evil did love of money bring to Glory?

7. Glory Community Church found itself the beneficiary of an enormous gift—yet many months went by before the church leaders thought of using some of the money to help needier churches. Do you have examples in your life where you might have exercised wiser stewardship of unexpected gifts you had received?

8. The job of reconciling the members of Glory Community Church fell to Reverend Daniel Hartman. How did he accomplish it?

9. How did Reverend Hartman's application of the wisdom contained in Philippians 4:2–3 help to put things right inside Glory Community Church?

10. Think of the times you have worked to reconcile people or groups of people (members of your family, for example). How did you do it? Did you succeed?

Love Inspired®

Celebrate Love Inspired's 10th anniversary with top authors and great stories all year long!

FOR HER SON'S LOVE

BY

KATHRYN SPRINGER

A Tiny Blessings Tale

Loving families and needy children continue to come together to fulfill God's greatest plans!

With the legality of her son's adoption in question, Miranda Jones knows she can't trust anyone in Chestnut Grove with her secrets—especially Andrew Noble. He was working his way into her heart, but his investigation into her past could tear her family apart.

Available July wherever you buy books.

Steeple
Hill®

REQUEST YOUR FREE BOOKS!

2 FREE RIVETING INSPIRATIONAL NOVELS
PLUS 2 FREE MYSTERY GIFTS

Love Inspired®
SUSPENSE

YES! Please send me 2 FREE Love Inspired® Suspense novels and my 2 FREE mystery gifts. After receiving them, if I don't wish to receive any more books, I can return the shipping statement marked "cancel." If I don't cancel, I will receive 4 brand-new novels every month and be billed just $3.99 per book in the U.S. or $4.74 per book in Canada, plus 25¢ shipping and handling per book and applicable taxes, if any*. That's a savings of 20% off the cover price! I understand that accepting the 2 free books and gifts places me under no obligation to buy anything. I can always return a shipment and cancel at any time. Even if I never buy another book from Steeple Hill, the two free books and gifts are mine to keep forever.

123 IDN EL5H   323 IDN ELQH

Name	(PLEASE PRINT)	
Address		Apt. #
City	State/Prov.	Zip/Postal Code

Signature (if under 18, a parent or guardian must sign)

Order online at www.LoveInspiredSuspense.com

Or mail to Steeple Hill Reader Service™:

IN U.S.A.: P.O. Box 1867, Buffalo, NY 14240-1867
IN CANADA: P.O. Box 609, Fort Erie, Ontario L2A 5X3

Not valid to current Love Inspired Suspense subscribers.

Want to try two free books from another series?
Call 1-800-873-8635 or visit www.morefreebooks.com

* Terms and prices subject to change without notice. NY residents add applicable sales tax. Canadian residents will be charged applicable provincial taxes and GST. This offer is limited to one order per household. All orders subject to approval. Credit or debit balances in a customer's account(s) may be offset by any other outstanding balance owed by or to the customer. Please allow 4 to 6 weeks for delivery.

Your Privacy: Steeple Hill is committed to protecting your privacy. Our Privacy Policy is available online at www.eHarlequin.com or upon request from the Reader Service. From time to time we make our lists of customers available to reputable firms who may have a product or service of interest to you. If you would prefer we not share your name and address, please check here.

LISUS07

Love Inspired SUSPENSE

TITLES AVAILABLE NEXT MONTH

Don't miss these four stories in July

NO LOVE LOST by Lynn Bulock
Cozy mystery

She married a murderer? Gracie Lee Harris was sure Hal,
her ex-husband, didn't have *that* dark a side. But with her ex
as the prime suspect in his fiancée's death and her boyfriend,
Ray Fernandez, as the lead investigator, Gracie could only pray
that Hal's secrets wouldn't get *her* killed!

DEATH BENEFITS by Hannah Alexander
A HIDEAWAY novel

Attending a wedding in Hawaii seemed the perfect tropical
dream to Ginger Carpenter...until an escaped convict began
stalking her young foster nieces. To protect them, she would
have to rely on Dr. Ray Clyde—the one man she never wanted to
see again.

VALLEY OF SHADOWS by Shirlee McCoy
A LAKEVIEW novel

Heartbroken following the death of her nephew, the last thing
Miranda Shelton expected was to become involved in a DEA
investigation. Yet now she and Agent Hawke Morran were
running for their lives, desperate to uncover the truth behind
the betrayal that brought them together.

DANGEROUS SECRETS by Lyn Cote
Harbor Intrigue

The town of Winfield's peacefulness was shattered by the bizarre
death of Sylvie Patterson's cousin. And as the last person to see
him alive, Sylvie was square in the sights of investigator Ridge
Matthews. But as another family member died and Ridge got
closer to the truth, they must learn to trust in each other—and
God—to uncover the deadly secrets lurking in her once quiet town.

LISCNM0607